A Contrite Heart

Also by Tom Milton
Milos and Amira
The Lost Summer
The Lineman
The Last Resort
The Godmother
Eden Valley
The Silver Locket
Orphans of War
Invisible Wounds
Leave of Absence
Outside the Gate
The Golden Door
Sara's Laughter
A Shower of Roses
Infamy
All the Flowers
The Admiral's Daughter
No Way to Peace

A Contrite Heart

Tom Milton

NEPPERHAN PRESS, LLC
YONKERS, NY

Copyright © Tom Milton, 2021

All rights reserved. No part of this book may be reproduced or transmitted in any form or by any means, electronic or mechanical, including photocopying, recording, or by any information storage and retrieval system, without written permission from the author, except for the inclusion of brief quotations in a review.

Published by Nepperhan Press, LLC
P.O. Box 1448, Yonkers, NY 10702
nepperhan@optonline.net
nepperhan.com

PUBLISHER'S NOTE

This is a work of fiction. Names, characters, places, and incidents are the product of the author's imagination or are used fictitiously, and any resemblance to actual persons, living or dead, events, or locales is entirely coincidental.

Printed in the United States of America

Library of Congress Control Number: 2021951805

ISBN 978-1-7377413-1-2

Cover art was licensed from Publitek, Inc.

For Marie

My sacrifice, O God, is a broken spirit.
A broken and contrite heart, O God,
you will not despise.
   Psalm 51:17

New York, 2002

ONE

AS SHE WAS leaving her apartment building Catalina confronted a young man standing on the sidewalk who, looking as if he knew her, said: "Martina Aguirre?"

Though the name pierced her heart with the memory of her crime, she managed to reply: "That's not my name. You have the wrong person."

"No, I don't. You responded to that name."

"You surprised me," she told him truthfully. "I would have responded to anything. So excuse me, I have to go to work."

"We need to talk."

"Well, I don't know you, and you don't know me, so we have nothing to talk about."

"We have a lot to talk about. But if you can't talk now, we can talk later. I'm not going away." From the way he spoke English he sounded like an Argentine who had learned the language with a British accent, as it was often taught in schools there. And that made her even more wary of him.

She turned away from him and started walking briskly toward Avenue A. She sensed that he was following her, so she walked faster, hoping that if she joined a stream of pedestrians he would leave her alone. When she reached the avenue she glanced back and didn't see him, which gave her some relief, though not much because he knew where she lived so he could always find her. He only had to wait for her to go home at the end of the day.

Heading toward 3rd Street, she wondered who he was. He might be an agent of the Argentine police, but ten years ago the Menem government gave amnesty to many of those who had been involved in the Dirty War, including some of the worst offenders, so it wasn't likely that they would pursue her. And the only people who knew the alias she had used in her crime were other members of her group, who had all been killed. So who was this guy? And what did he want from her?

At 3rd Street she headed east, and following her usual routine she reached the church of Most Holy Redeemer. She paused to gaze up at the imposing façade of gray stone and the tower above, and then she entered, awed by the spacious interior with its white columns that rose and branched into red and gold decorated arches, up to the blue vaulted ceilings. The church was filled with light, filtered through stained-glass windows that were imported from Germany more than a hundred years ago. At that time the church was the heart of a community known as Little Germany, and it was regarded as their cathedral. Now it was still an active church, with a diverse group of parishioners.

Catalina didn't attend daily Mass, but she did stop here every morning on her way to work, and more than usual today she needed what the church offered her. She stopped at a back pew, genuflected, sat on the bench, leaned over, and pulled back the kneeler, which made a sound landing on the floor that echoed in the empty space. She knelt down and bowed her head and began as usual with words from the Miserere: "Have mercy on me, O God, according to your merciful love. According to your abundant mercy, blot out my transgressions. Wash me thoroughly from my iniquity, and cleanse me from my sin. For I know my iniquity, and my sin is ever before me. My sacrifice, O God, is a broken spirit. A broken and contrite heart, O God, you will not despise."

After praying for about twenty minutes she rose from the pew, raised the kneeler, and headed back toward the main entrance. She was intercepted by Father Benicio, who must have spotted her, knowing her routine. He was an assistant pastor at the church, having arrived there freshly ordained several months ago. He had come to New York with his family at the age of ten, fleeing the war in El Salvador, so he understood her background. And being her confessor, he knew what she had done.

"*Hola, padre,*" she greeted him.

"*Hola, Catalina,*" he said, looking at her compassionately. "*Te ves preocupada.*"

"Yes, father, I *am* worried. I just ran into someone who—" She paused to find an appropriate word. "—stirred things up."

"Was it someone you know?"

She shook her head. "I don't know who it was, but he knew me. I mean he knew the alias I used in my crime."

"How did he find you?"

"I don't know. At first I thought he was a police agent, but after all these years, why would they come after me?"

"Some people never forget," the priest told her. "And never forgive."

"Well, whatever he wants, I'll have to deal with it."

"I understand. But if I can help you, let me know. If he wants to talk with you, maybe I could mediate."

"Thanks, father."

He gave her a blessing before she turned to go, and she left the church feeling better, though not cleansed.

Outside, she searched up and down the street, but she didn't see the guy. She hoped she wouldn't see him again until she went home after work, and maybe by then she would be in a better position to deal with him.

She walked a few blocks north on Avenue A, passing the usual mix of people ranging from the homeless in soiled rags to young professionals in designer clothes. The latter were a sign of the gradual gentrification of the neighborhood, which for most of its history had been a haven for immigrants, including Germans, Italians, Eastern European Jews, Poles, Ukrainians, and Hispanics. By now it was no longer affordable for immigrants, who were more likely to settle in the Bronx, Mount Vernon, and Yonkers. Though immigrants and their families were being driven out of the old buildings by rising rents, there were remnants of them, especially Hispanics, who were still the dominant group among Catalina's patients.

She turned into the street where she had her practice. It was on the ground floor of an old four-story building in a block that evidently hadn't yet been targeted by developers, so the rent was still affordable. She had the whole floor, with a waiting room, an office, and two examination rooms. She arrived at five minutes after nine, a few minutes later than usual because of the encounter in front of her apartment building, but in plenty of time for her first appointment.

Tonia, her nurse, was sitting at the reception desk, talking on the phone. It sounded like she was booking an appointment for a patient, so Catalina greeted her with a friendly wave and continued into her office, which had a basic metal desk, a sofa, a chair, and file cabinets. On the wall opposite the desk were her diploma from New York University and her certificate of residency in internal medicine at New York University Hospital. There wasn't a diploma from the medical school at the University of Buenos Aires, though there should have been because she had completed all the courses required for her degree there, but at this point in her life it wouldn't have much value professionally, so it wasn't worth the risk of asking someone there to dig up her record.

She had just sat down behind her desk when Tonia appeared in the doorway, looking good as usual. Today she was wearing a bright pink summer dress, her dark hair tied back neatly, and her face made up expertly. She was the daughter of a Puerto Rican farm laborer who had come to New York in the early 1950s and raised a family of three children, living in a project on Avenue D. Tonia was the youngest, the only girl, and by now she had raised a family of her own, with two adult children living in Yonkers, where housing was more affordable. Tonia still lived a few blocks away in the rent-controlled apartment where her children had grown up, and she had the whole place to herself because her husband had drifted away.

"*Buenos días, doctora*," Tonia said. "*Como está?*"

"*Muy bien*," Catalina said. "*Y tú?*"

"*Muy bien, gracias a Dios*. I have your schedule of appointments for today." Tonia advanced to the desk and handed her a sheet of paper.

After looking at the list Catalina said: "Did Mr. Hagos confirm his appointment?"

"Yes, he called a few minutes before you got here. He doesn't have any health insurance."

"That's okay." Most of her patients were on Medicaid, some were on Medicare, and almost none had private insurance. About one in ten of her patients had no insurance of any kind, so Catalina didn't charge them. While that took care of her services, it didn't cover prescription drugs, but she used a prescription assistance program to pay for them.

"Oh, I meant to ask you," Tonia said. "My daughter has an offer from a school in Yonkers, and I wonder if your daughter knows anything about the school."

Catalina had heard from Tonia that her daughter wasn't happy at the elementary school in a Westchester suburb where she worked because so many of the students were spoiled and their parents were disrespectful, maybe because she wasn't white. Catalina's daughter Lucía taught at an elementary school in the inner city of Yonkers, where almost sixty percent of her students were Hispanic, mostly Dominicans and Mexicans. "Sure. What school is it?"

Tonia gave her the name of the school. It wasn't the school where Lucía taught, which was the only school in Yonkers that Catalina knew, so she agreed to ask her daughter about it. They resumed reviewing the appointments for today, and then Tonia went back to her desk, where she also served as receptionist and office manager. After so many years of working at a hospital and in a doctor's office, she could do everything short of surgery.

For a while after Tonia left her office Catalina brooded about the encounter, remembering events that most of the time were buried under the activities of her daily life. Occasionally she had flashbacks of things that had happened in Argentina while she was doing her residency. At least so far she had escaped from the vengeance of the military government, but she hadn't escaped from the memory of what she had done. And feeling the chronic pain of her guilt, she fervently prayed to the framed image of Our Lady of Luján on her desk.

She was brought back to the present by a light rap on her door, which meant that her first patient had arrived. She didn't have to do anything yet because Tonia would have him fill out the standard questionnaire and then take him into an examining room, where she would do his vital signs, but Catalina had to prepare herself mentally to serve the patient. Whatever else was on her mind, she had to clear it and give the patient her full attention.

While waiting for Tonia she reviewed her list of patients for the day. The patient with Tonia at the moment had been referred by the Catholic Worker, which she had gotten involved with as a member of a community group whose mission was to help the poor in the neighborhood and to prevent them from being driven out by gentrification. Over the years she had volunteered her services as a doctor at the Catholic Worker, and she maintained a role in their mission by treating patients they referred to her. These patients were often homeless, often with histories of mental illness or drug abuse, though the underlying problem they had in common was poverty. She knew about poverty from having worked as a volunteer in the *villas miseria* of Buenos Aires, and from her experience there and here she had learned that there were no fundamental differences between the poor in Argentina and the poor in America. Wherever you found it, poverty was poverty, and its effects on people were the same.

With a rap before opening the door, Tonia returned in a crisp white lab coat. Looking concerned, she handed Catalina the patient's paperwork and said: "*Su presión arterial es muy alta.* It's one seventy-five over one ten."

"*De veras?* That's not good." She took the papers from Tonia and perused them. She noted that the patient wasn't on any medication and hadn't ever had surgery, but he was only thirty so he should have been in good health. He had complained of headaches, dizziness, breathing problems, and blurring vision, which made sense. And he was a smoker.

"I think we should give him an EKG," Tonia said.

"Yes, we should. You can do that after I examine him." Catalina got up from her desk and put on the lab coat that was draped over the back of her chair, and she followed Tonia out through the waiting room and down the corridor to the room where the patient was waiting.

A CONTRITE HEART

Opening the door, she saw a lean dark man sitting on the examining table with his head drooped and his shoulders hunched. "Mr. Hagos? I'm Dr. Rinaldi."

"Hello, doctor," he said, looking surprised that the doctor was a woman. He was an attractive man, with warm brown eyes, a sensitive mouth, and closely cut hair.

Since she had heard a foreign accent, she asked: "Where are you from?"

"Eritrea," he said humbly.

"Where in Eritrea?"

"A village not far from Seghendeyti. It is near the border with Ethiopia."

"There's a war there, right?" she said, having read about it in the *New York Times*.

He nodded sadly. "Yes, there is."

Based on her instincts, Catalina asked: "Are you a refugee from that war?"

He hesitated, evidently wondering if he could trust her, and finally said: "Yes, I am waiting for asylum in this country."

She knew about the process of getting asylum, having suffered through it twenty-five years ago. She remembered the fear of being deported to Argentina, where she would be captured, tortured, and killed. And she understood why this young man would have high blood pressure. "Tell me about it."

He looked blank.

"Tell me what happened to you there."

Slowly, in his broken English he told her how his village was bombed and eventually obliterated by the Ethiopian army. He lost his parents and every other member of his family, except for his wife and two children, whom he had rescued from his burning house. With the help of Catholic Relief Services he had brought his family to New York, where he found a job as a mechanic. They lived in a project on Avenue D.

"So how long have you been here?"

"Almost a year. And we still have not been given asylum."

"Is anyone helping you with the process?"

"The church is helping us."

"Well, from what I've read, I think you'll get asylum. Your case just has to work its way through the bureaucracy."

She asked him to take off his shirt so that she could listen to his heart and his breathing. She noticed that he wore a plain wooden cross around his neck on a brown cord, which together with his having been helped by Catholic Relief Services and his being referred by the Catholic Worker, indicated that he was a Catholic. On his back was a scar from a major burn, but apart from that he was in good shape, without an ounce of fat on his well-toned torso. His heart was pounding, though that could have been for a number of reasons, and his breathing wasn't smooth. But she would need more information before making a diagnosis and deciding how to treat him.

"You smoke, right?" she said as he was putting his shirt back on.

He nodded. "Yes."

"How much?"

He shrugged. "A pack a day."

"Well, I know it's easier said than done, but you have to quit smoking. It's bad for your health in many ways, but you have very high blood pressure, and it's contributing to that."

"What does it mean high blood pressure?"

"It means that the force of blood flowing through your system is too high. And among other things it can lead to heart failure, stroke, kidney failure, vision loss, and sexual dysfunction." She believed in hitting patients hard with the facts of how a health problem could affect them. "So you have to control your blood pressure."

"How can I do that?"

"You can quit smoking. I'll also prescribe a treatment for you, depending on a test my nurse will give you."

"What test?"

"It's a test that records the electrical signals in your heart. It's called an electrocardiogram," she added, "or EKG for short."

"Okay," he said, though he looked dubious.

"How old are your children?"

"Three and five."

"Are they boys or girls?"

"A boy and a girl."

"Do you want to see your children grow up?"

"Yes, I do." There was a hint of tears in his brown eyes.

"Then you have to control your blood pressure."

"Okay," he said with conviction now.

"I'll treat you, and I'll also pray for you. Tell me who you pray to."

"What do you mean?"

"I pray to Our Lady of Luján," she told him. "That's because I'm from Argentina, and like you I came here as a refugee. So I know what it's like, and I want to help you however I can, with science and with faith."

He looked at her in amazement and said: "I pray to Our Lady of the Rosary."

"So I'll pray for you to Our Lady of the Rosary. And now my nurse will give you an EKG. Okay?"

He nodded. "Okay."

On the way back to her office she noticed an old woman in the waiting area with features that suggested a Mexican or Central American heritage. She was reminded of the people she treated in the *villas miseria,* many of whom came from northern Argentina or Bolivia or Paraguay, with brown skin and indigenous features that distinguished them from the mainly white European people of central Buenos Aires. You rarely saw those other people on the city streets, so you would never guess they were there.

In her office Catalina sat down at her desk and made notes on Mr. Hagos. Based on what she had seen so far, she would probably give him a diuretic and see if that helped. She would have him come back in two weeks. And she would pray to Our Lady of the Rosary for his family to be granted asylum.

By six o'clock they were done with the last patient, and Tonia had gone home. Catalina lingered in her office, reflecting on the events of the day and looking forward to dinner with an old friend, whom she was going to meet at seven. Remembering Tonia's question about the school in Yonkers, she decided to call her daughter.

Catalina had a close relationship with her daughter. They had shared a bedroom until Lucía was almost nine, living with Uncle Angelo and Aunt Elda, who had given her a safe haven when she arrived as a refugee from Argentina, two months pregnant. As soon as the opportunity arose she moved to her own apartment, which was right across the hall from the apartment of her uncle and aunt. It wasn't rent-controlled like theirs but it was rent-stabilized, which limited increases in the rent and enabled her to pursue her mission instead of having to make more money. Lucía went to the local public schools and earned a bachelor's degree in English from Hunter College, followed by a master's in education. Upon being certified by the state she received job offers from schools in Manhattan, the Bronx, and Yonkers. She was tempted to take the job in Manhattan and continue living at home, but after talking it over they agreed that it was time for Lucía to separate from her mother, so she took the job in Yonkers.

Last summer Catalina helped her find an apartment that was only ten minutes by bus from the school where she would be teaching, and she helped her furnish it, shopping around at local stores. With its diversity of immigrants Yonkers reminded her of the East Village before gentrification began, so she was glad that her daughter had chosen the school there. And Lucía loved teaching at the school. She had a class of third-grade students whose families were struggling economically and were doing jobs that other people wouldn't think of doing. Most of the students spoke Spanish at home, so it was very useful for Lucía to be bilingual, though having learned Spanish from her mother she spoke the language with a different accent from her students. Within a few weeks she made a friend, a fourth-grade teacher whose family had immigrated from the Dominican Republic and lived in a neighborhood where there were a lot of Dominicans. The friend, whose name was Noemi, was still living at home, and it wasn't long before she invited Lucía to have Sunday dinner with her family, which from then on gave Lucía an alternative to spending the weekend with her mother. Noemi had an extended family, and early that spring she introduced Lucía to a cousin, who became Lucía's first boyfriend. His name was Danilo, and he taught math at a Yonkers high school. He was five years older than Lucía, but he was still living at home in the same neighborhood as Noemi. After hearing so much about him Catalina finally met him, and she liked him, though she worried about Lucía getting too close to him too soon. She worried because at the same age she had fallen in love with Lucía's father.

She reached for the phone and punched Lucía's number. After three rings she wondered if Lucía was out for the evening, but then on the fourth ring Lucía answered.

"Mom?" Lucía guessed.

"Yeah, hi, sweetie. I hope I didn't catch you at a bad time."

"No, I was just checking a pasta recipe."

"What kind of pasta?"

"Pasta with bolognese sauce. I'm having company," Lucía added.

"Oh? That's nice." Catalina refrained from asking who the company was.

"It's Danilo," her daughter told her, answering her unasked question. "It's his favorite pasta, so I hope I do it right. He can be picky about his food."

This observation indicated that the relationship had at least gone a certain distance. "Are you using ground beef?"

"Yeah. They had a mixture of beef, pork, and veal, but that sounded complicated."

"With ground beef make sure you cook it with onion, garlic, and tomato, all together. That way the meat won't dry out. What kind of pasta are you using?"

"Penne, like you use."

"Then be sure to take it out of the pot before it's soft and finish it in the pan with the sauce."

"Okay. His mother's Italian, *viste?*"

"I thought he was Dominican."

"He is, but they have Italians in that country too. They have more Spaniards, so they don't speak Spanish like we do."

"Well, no one speaks Spanish like we do."

After a pause Lucía said: "I can tell by the way they speak English where people are from. I mean, last spring there was a girl in my class from Kosovo, and when I ran into a kid in the hall who had the same accent, I guessed where he was from."

"If you can do that," Catalina said, proud of her daughter, "you have a good ear."

"Yeah, maybe I should learn another language."

"What language would you learn?"

"I don't know. Everyone says we should learn Chinese."

"If I learned another language, I think it would be African. I'm seeing more patients from Africa now."

"What countries are they from?"

"Today I had a patient from Eritrea. Luckily, he spoke English."

"Aren't they having a war with another country?"

"They're having a war with Ethiopia, and he's a refugee from that war. He lost his home and all of his family except his wife and his children. My heart went out to him."

"I have two students who are refugees. One's from Honduras, and the other's from El Salvador. They're refugees from gang wars in those countries."

"What about the gangs in the neighborhood of your school?"

"Oh, they're not having wars now," Lucía said. "They're only mugging people."

Remembering the reason for her phone call, Catalina said: "Speaking of schools, Tonia's daughter has an offer from a school in Yonkers, and she asked me if you know anything about the school."

"Which school is it?"

Catalina told her.

"That's like our school. It has the same kind of students."

"Is it a good school?"

"Yeah, it is."

"So I can recommend it to her?"

"Yeah, if that's what her daughter wants."

"I think it's what her daughter wants. She's not happy where she is now."

"Well, I'm happy where I am now," Lucía said. "And thank you, mom, for encouraging me to take this job."

That made Catalina feel good. She ended the call a few minutes later, saying: "I know you'll cook a good dinner. *Te amo.*"

After locking the outer door of the office she headed toward Avenue A and continued to First Avenue, where she was meeting Rachel at a Peruvian chicken restaurant. Rachel was literally an old friend, in her late eighties. She had really been a friend of Angelo and Elda, who joined her in campaigns to save the neighborhood. Rachel had worked on such campaigns with Jane Jacobs, whose movement had prevented Robert Moses from running a freeway through the heart of Greenwich Village. And for years she had been working to save the East Village from gentrification. She made a living from the literary agency that she had founded in the late 1930s. She claimed it was the only remaining leftist agency in New York, and like other agencies its income came mainly from a few titles that had done well and were still in print. Her most notable title was a leftist textbook that was still used by political science departments of universities.

Rachel had grown up in the neighborhood, the daughter of a man who ran a popular Yiddish theater, which later became an off-off-Broadway theater. Her grandfather, an immigrant from Ukraine, had been a doctrinaire communist, and leftism continued to flow in her family's blood from one generation to the next, with her daughter being a leftist journalist who regularly attacked the Bush administration for policies that favored the rich. With a communist grandfather and a socialist father, Catalina had a similar family background, and she had a similar mission, though she pursued it in a different way.

The restaurant was on First Avenue, and it was Rachel's favorite place. For less than ten dollars you could get a meal of a half roast chicken, rice, and beans including a soft drink. It had simple Formica tables that were packed together and rearrangeable at the whims of the diners, depending on the size of their group. A wonderful aroma, which included garlic, greeted Catalina when she entered the restaurant, and there was Rachel at a table near the window, sipping water through a straw. She was wearing a plain beige dress which below its neckline was ornamented by a large white button with black letters that said: "TAX THE RICH."

"*Hola, doctora*," Rachel said with a wave of her hand. It was customary for them to greet each other in Spanish, which they had been doing since Catalina was introduced to Rachel by Angelo as his niece from Argentina. Rachel had learned some Spanish from living in the neighborhood, but with Catalina she never used Spanish beyond the words of greeting. Catalina had once heard her talking with the woman who ran the local bodega, and she had been impressed by Rachel's command of the language for food and prices.

"*Hola, Raquel.*" Sitting down at the table across from her, Catalina noticed that Rachel looked essentially the same as when they had met more than twenty years ago. Her hair was still wavy and reddish blond, and her green eyes were still as bright as ever. Only her skin looked older, but you would never guess she was in her late eighties. "How are you doing?"

"I'm doing fine. We just won a battle against a developer."

"Really? That's great. What kind of battle?"

"A zoning battle. We stopped him from building towers with luxury condominiums. At least for a while," Rachel added.

"You mean the war isn't over."

"No. The war will never be over until we have a government of the people, by the people, and for the people."

"That sounds familiar."

"It was said by Abraham Lincoln, who didn't live to implement his vision."

At that moment a waiter stopped at their table. He looked Mexican, and the guy running the place was Dominican. Catalina had learned on their initial dinner at the restaurant that "Peruvian" was a marketing term to differentiate the place.

"Are you having the usual?" she asked Rachel.

"Oh, yes." To the waiter Rachel said: "I'll have the half roast chicken with rice and beans."

"Red or black beans?" the waiter asked.
"Red beans. I always have red beans."
"And you?" the waiter asked her.
"I'll have the same, but I don't need the soft drink. Just give me water, please."

When the waiter had left to fill their order they exchanged the latest information about their daughters, as they always did. And that lasted until the waiter brought their food. While occupied with eating they didn't talk much, but after they had finished, with Rachel reserving half of her food to take home, Catalina mentioned the young man who had accosted her that morning. Rachel knew her whole story, so Catalina didn't have to explain.

"He didn't identify himself?" Rachel said.
"I didn't ask him to."
"Well, if you see him again, make him identify himself. If he's police, he should show you a badge or something."
"Okay. But what if he's not police?"
"Hm. If he's not police, who else could have found you after all these years?"
"I don't know. What worries me is that he said he isn't going away. So he could be waiting for me when I get home."
"Then maybe you should tell the police he's stalking you."

She imagined what might happen if she got the police involved, and she shook her head, saying: "I don't want to do that. It would complicate things."

Rachel nodded as if she understood. "You know, at times like this it would be nice to have a big male around."
"Yeah, it would be nice."
"If Angelo was still around, he'd deal with this guy."

Angelo, who could lift iron and steel and stone for his gigantic sculptures, had been a big male. "Yeah, he would."
"I miss him."
"I do too. He was like a second father to me when I needed one most."

After a respectful moment of silence Rachel said: "So you don't know any big males who could scare this guy away?"

"No. I don't even know any big females."

"Then be careful, okay? If he wants to talk, stay out on the street. Don't even think about letting him into your building."

"I won't," she promised.

Because it was summer it was still light when Catalina turned into her street after walking Rachel home, and at first she didn't see the guy. But then he emerged, getting up from the steps of the adjacent building where he had been sitting, and he approached her silently.

She faced him, saying: "If you don't leave me alone, I'll call the police."

"Call them," he said, stopping just beyond her personal space. "I'll tell them what you did in Argentina."

"I don't know what you're talking about. Who are you?"

"I'm the grandson of Colonel Yribarren."

So he wasn't a police agent. He had tracked her down for another reason. "What do you want?"

"I want justice," he told her simply.

"Well, that has nothing do with me," she insisted, about to turn away from him.

"It has everything to do with you." In the fading light he edged toward her, a dark shadow that had come for retribution. "If I kill you, I'll have justice."

Catalina understood, and she braced herself for his next move.

TWO

CATALINA HAD JUST started her fifth year of medical school at the University of Buenos Aires when her life changed radically. Until then she had single-mindedly pursued her dream of being a doctor, ignoring the events that disrupted her country. She lived with her parents in Flores, a middle-class neighborhood about twenty minutes by subway from the city center. Their house was more than large enough to accommodate her immediate family, which included her younger brother Marco. Her grandparents had lived with them until they passed away during her last two years of high school. They had immigrated from Italy to Argentina early in the century, coming from Naples, recently married, and settling in La Boca, where her grandfather worked as a laborer in the port and her grandmother worked as a seamstress in a sweatshop. They raised five children, the youngest of whom was Catalina's father, and he was the only one of their children who went to college, commuting from La Boca, working part time, and eventually earning a law degree from the University of Buenos Aires.

After doing well at a prominent law firm her father, whose name was Santino, established his own practice in which instead of serving banks and corporations he served families and small businesses. By his early thirties he was in a position financially to marry the woman who worked as his legal secretary and to buy a house in Flores. At the time his parents didn't want to live with him, not only because they were deeply rooted in their neighborhood but also because his father, a communist, hadn't forgiven him for serving capitalists. His father felt that he had betrayed the working class, and there wasn't a reconciliation between them until Santino developed a practice serving more acceptable clients. Even after her grandparents moved into the apartment that her father had reserved for them, Catalina at an early age was aware of the tension between her father and her grandfather, who felt that as a Peronist her father wasn't far enough to the left. Their arguments were especially heated on the subject of Perón, who was president of the country at that time. Her father regarded Perón as a champion of the working class, while her grandfather regarded him as a fascist. Taking the obtuse position that the enemy of his enemy was his friend, her grandfather cheered when the military overthrew Perón, even though the generals were definitely fascists. Catalina was only three at the time, but it wasn't long before she was able to understand their arguments and get an education in politics.

In addition to being a communist her grandfather was an atheist who never joined her grandmother and their children when they went to church in La Boca. Her father emerged from that household as an agnostic, but he was brought back into the church by her mother, a devout Catholic who went to daily Mass at the Basílica San José de Flores. In fact, it was her mother who helped her father unite his politics and his faith in a mission to help the downtrodden. Her parents agreed that Perón had done a lot to help the working class, though her mother gave more credit to Eva, whom she regarded as a saint. Like Eva her mother grew up in a province and came to Buenos Aires as a young woman to pursue a career. Unlike Eva she didn't grow up poor, but she had limited prospects in Rio Cuarto, so she left home and enrolled in a school to develop skills as a secretary, which led to a job and eventually to a marriage. Her mother, who was practical, was a perfect complement to her father, who was an idealist.

During her years of elementary school Catalina lived under the elected governments of Arturo Frondizi and Arturo Illia. Like other members of his party, her father questioned the legitimacy of those governments because the Peronists weren't allowed to field a candidate in the elections. The military overthrew Frondizi before the end of his term, and they engineered the election of Illia, whom they also overthrew. So all through school and through her first four years of medical school Catalina had lived under governments that either owed their existence to the military or were military juntas. This situation troubled her father, and by then it troubled her grandfather, so the political gap between them was bridged by their common hatred of the military. Catalina listened to their long discussions, continuing her education in politics, but those discussions ended when her grandfather died, and by then she had no interest in politics, being fully occupied by her courses at the medical school.

Catalina was a good student, though she was challenged by the courses in chemistry, so until she got through them she had little time for anything but studying. She certainly had no time for boys, and she avoided social activities that included them. She did have a friend, Olivia, who also lived in Flores, and they commuted to the university together on most days, taking the subway from San José de Flores to Plaza Miserere and from there transferring to the line that stopped at the Córdoba station, which was walking distance from the medical school. When there were exams they studied together. Olivia was better at chemistry, and Catalina was better at biology, so they were able to help each other. They socialized together in the neighborhood, but they were both committed to their studies, and their friendship carried them into their fifth year of medical school.

By then the military, unable to govern the country, had allowed elections. The presidency was won by Héctor Cámpora, a left-wing Peronist and presumed stand-in for Perón, who wasn't allowed to run himself. In those elections Catalina's father ran as a candidate of the Peronist party for the Chamber of Deputies, and he won with a solid majority. He still regarded Perón as a champion of the working class, and he was positioned on the left wing of the party. His father was no longer around to prod him further to the left, but as things developed he was already too far left for the people who took over the party. When Perón returned in June of 1973 after eighteen years of exile he was greeted at Ezeiza Airport by thousands of supporters from the left and right wings of the party, but snipers positioned by the right wing opened fire on supporters from the left wing, including members of the Peronist Youth and the Montoneros, killing at least thirty people and wounding at least four hundred people. It was known as the Ezeiza Massacre, and it alerted Catalina's father to the fact that his leftist views no longer represented the mainstream of the party. Disillusioned, he admitted to Catalina that his father had been right about Perón.

For the next year the violence between the left and right wings of the party escalated, and after Perón died in July of 1974 it got even worse. Though his wife Isabel, who had been vice president, became president, the de facto head of the government was her adviser, José López Rega, whose death squad known as the Triple A was systematically eliminating leftists. By the time Catalina started her fifth year of medical school in March of 1975 the level of political violence in the country was higher than ever, with left-wing and right-wing terrorists killing each other as well as a lot of innocent people.

One morning, while they were on their way to the medical school, Olivia told her about a meeting of a student group that had invited a well-known priest as a speaker. His name was Francisco Muñoa, and he was the mentor of Young Catholic Students, an international organization whose mission was to make students more aware of their social responsibilities and to help them maintain their faith. Since the meeting was after their last class, and since its purpose sounded like it would meet with approval of both her parents, Catalina was in favor of attending, so in the late afternoon she and Olivia were sitting in a room with about twenty people their age, mostly girls. When the speaker entered the room walking circumspectly behind the student leader of the group, the girls twittered, and Catalina could understand why. The priest was a tall man in his mid-thirties with a handsome face and heavenly blue eyes, and though she didn't allow herself to twitter, her heart throbbed in anticipation.

The leader introduced him as Father Francisco and gave a brief biography, including the fact that he was born in Buenos Aires and earned a degree in literature from the University of Buenos Aires before pursuing his vocation as a priest. After studying in France he returned with a mission of helping the poor, and he was assigned to a parish in Almagro. Meanwhile, he taught theology at the university and mentored a group of Young Catholic Students.

A CONTRITE HEART

Several years ago he built a church in a *villa miseria*, south of Flores, to serve the poorest inhabitants of the city, which didn't endear him to the hierarchy of the church. The church in the *villa* was called Cristo Libertador.

Catalina understood why the hierarchy would oppose godless leftists but not why it would oppose religious leftists because, whatever their politics, they were carrying out the church's mission to help the poor. So even before Father Francisco started speaking she had a question for him.

The priest, who had been seated in a folding chair like all of them, got up as they applauded and stood before them, looking around and resting his eyes on them individually. Then after a suspenseful silence he said: "Well, that was quite an introduction. I learned from it that my building a church in a *villa miseria* didn't endear me to the hierarchy of the church. And I guess it didn't. But one of my missions is teaching, and I hope I can teach some things to people who already know everything."

There was mild laughter.

"If any of you are Catholics, please raise your hands."

Almost all of the students raised a hand.

"That's good to see. Do you know what it means to be a Catholic?"

There was silence.

"It means fundamentally to obey the two great commandments that our Lord gave us. Can anyone tell me the first commandment?"

A few girls raised their hands.

"Yes," he said, looking at one of them. "Your name is?"

"Graciela," the girl said.

"Graciela," he said gently, "can you tell us the first great commandment?"

After clearing her throat the girl said: "You shall love the Lord your God with all your heart, and with all your soul, and with all your mind."

"Excellent. Are you sure you're not a Protestant? They read the Bible more than we do."

There was some laughter.

"So what's the second great commandment?"

Finding the necessary courage, Catalina raised her hand, and gazing at her with his heavenly blue eyes, the priest said: "Your name is?"

"Catalina," she managed to say.

"Catalina, can you tell us the second great commandment?"

"You shall love your neighbor as yourself."

"Excellent. You're a great group. God bless you."

They waited for him to continue.

Moving among them, the priest said: "Now, both of those commandments are about love, so we need to know what love is. Can anyone tell me what love is?"

The girl directly in front of Catalina raised her hand.

"Your name is?"

"Sylvia."

"Sylvia, can you tell us what love is?"

"Love is wanting what's good for another."

"Excellent. Love in this sense is not about *wanting* another, though I know that kind of love is on your minds occasionally." There were some giggles. "It's wanting what's good for another, as Sylvia said. But love isn't only about wanting, it's also about doing. In other words, love isn't only a feeling, it's action."

"What kind of action do you mean?" a boy asked.

Turning to him, the priest asked: "What kind of action do you think I mean?"

"I don't know. I guess it's doing things for other people."

"Exactly. And let's be clear. I don't mean political action, I mean personal action."

"Why not political action?" the same boy asked.

"Political action," the priest said sadly, "is what's tearing our country apart. We have people on both the left and the right who believe that any kind of action is justified in achieving their goals. The result is violence, which is never justified. If you love your neighbors as yourself, you don't kill them."

"If they try to kill you," the boy asked, "don't you have to defend yourself?"

"You can defend yourself, but killing them is not an acceptable way of defending yourself. There are other ways."

"Like what?" the boy persisted.

"Like getting them to understand why killing you won't solve the problem."

"Wouldn't that be difficult?"

"Of course it would be difficult. Doing the right thing is often difficult while doing the wrong thing is all too easy. If you have a gun, it's easy to kill someone. You just pull the trigger, and bang, they're dead. But how does that solve problems?"

There was a silence.

"The solution is love. As St. John of the Cross said, 'Where there is no love, put love—and you will find love.'"

Again there was a silence.

"So let's talk about personal action," the priest said, and he described the kind of things that Young Catholic Students were doing to promote social justice and peace.

When he concluded he invited any students who wanted to volunteer for such actions to put their names on a list that was on a table at the front of the room. Whatever it was, something made Catalina decide to put her name on the list, and she asked Olivia if she wanted to join her. Olivia hesitated, saying she wanted to think about it. So Catalina went by herself to the front of the room and put her name, address, and phone number on the list. In the space for her field of study she wrote that she was a medical student.

"Thank you, Catalina," the priest said, which helped to make her feel she had done the right thing in volunteering. It also gave her an opportunity to ask her question.

"Father," she said, "why didn't your building a church in a *villa miseria* endear you to the hierarchy of the church?"

He smiled. "That's a good question. I think because they're so afraid that what I'm doing promotes Marxism."

"But there's a difference between Marxism and the mission of the church to serve the poor. And if I can see the difference, why can't they?"

"Another good question. Maybe they can't see the difference because they're blinded by fear."

"Well, it's not good that the church is divided on this issue. We already have enough divisions in this country."

"Yes, we do. We have more than enough divisions." After glancing at the list he said: "So you're a medical student. Why do you want to be a doctor?"

"To help people."

"God bless you," he said. "I hope to see you working with us."

Outside in the hall she joined Olivia, who was talking with a big girl in a conservative dress. The girl was explaining something to Olivia, who politely interrupted her to introduce Catalina, saying: "Faustina, this is my friend Catalina."

"*Mucho gusto*," Catalina said, extending her hand.

"*Igualmente*," Faustina said. Her sandy hair was drawn back, and her green eyes peered through tortoise shell glasses. "I noticed that you put your name on Father Francisco's list."

"So?" Catalina said, wondering why it mattered to this girl.

"Before you get involved with him, there are some things you should know about him."

Though she was annoyed, Catalina was open to hearing what the girl had to say, and she had told her mother not to expect her home for dinner, so she had time to hear it.

"Let's go and have a coffee," Olivia suggested.

They left the building and walked down the street to a coffee shop where students hung out. They found a table in a back corner and sat down. After a waiter had taken their order, Catalina asked the girl: "Are you a medical student?"

"No. I'm getting a degree in theology."

"At this university?"

"No. At Catholic University."

"Why a degree in theology?" Olivia asked.

"I'm a lay teacher at a Catholic high school, so it'll be useful."

"Okay," Catalina said. "So what are some things I should know about Father Francisco?"

Before the girl could say anything Olivia said: "I hope he doesn't fool around with girls. I mean, he's so attractive, *viste?*"

Faustina shook her head. "No. That's not the problem."

"So what's the problem?" Catalina asked, beginning to lose patience.

"He preaches and practices liberation theology."

"What's that?"

"It's a heresy that emerged in Brazil and spread to the rest of Latin America." Faustina made it sound like a disease.

"But what is it?"

"It's a fusion of Marxism with the teachings of the church."

"What do you mean?"

"Marxism believes in class struggle, and liberation theology links that belief with the church's mission to help the poor, so the priests who practice liberation theology are political activists."

"What's wrong with political activists?" Catalina said, thinking of her father.

"There's nothing wrong up to a point," Faustina said, "but beyond that point they go against the teachings of the church."

"Can you give us an example?" Olivia asked.

"Sure, I can. There was a priest in Colombia whose name was Camilo Torres. Like Father Francisco he practiced liberation theology, he was very good looking, and he mentored students at the university. But after trying without success to bring about social change through peaceful methods he decided that violence was the only way. He became a guerrilla and fought in the war against the government. He said that if Jesus was alive today, he would be a guerrilla."

"But that's not Father Francisco," Catalina objected. "Father Francisco said that love is the solution, not violence."

"So did Father Torres—until he changed his mind. And I can give you another example. You know the Montoneros?"

"Yeah." They were a guerrilla movement that had declared war on the military government by kidnapping and killing General Aramburu, who was president not long after the overthrow of Perón. It happened during Catalina's senior year of high school, and her father told her it was revenge for a massacre of left-wing Peronists ordered by General Aramburu.

"And you know that Father Francisco has been the mentor of Young Catholic Students?"

"Yeah." She didn't see where this was going.

"Well, the leaders of the Montoneros came from his Young Catholic Students."

"Even if they did," Catalina said, not wanting to believe it, "he didn't teach them to use violence."

"Whatever he taught them, it led to violence."

"But that doesn't make him responsible for what they're doing. I mean, if I commit a murder, my parents aren't responsible."

"If you commit a murder," Faustina said, "your parents must have failed in some way."

"I don't agree," Olivia said. "Our parents aren't responsible for all the stupid things we do. We have free will, and we always have a choice."

"But our parents and our priests have choices as to which paths they open for us. And based on the actions of the people who have followed the path of liberation theology, we have to conclude that it can lead to violence."

"Maybe it can," Catalina said. "But it doesn't have to. As my friend said, we always have a choice. And if we decide to commit an act of violence, then we're responsible. We can't blame it on our parents, our teachers, or our priests."

Faustina smiled at her ruefully. "We do have a choice. So I felt it was my duty to warn you about Father Francisco."

"Okay. You warned me." Catalina finished her coffee and asked the waiter for the check. She didn't say another word until they had parted with Faustina, and then she said: "Explain why I don't like that girl."

"You don't like her," Olivia said as they headed for the subway station, "because she tried to pull Father Francisco down from his pedestal."

"He didn't put himself on a pedestal."

"He didn't, but you did."

When she got home she ate the dinner her mother had saved for her, sitting at the kitchen table with both of her parents. She told them about the meeting with Father Francisco and about her volunteering to support his work to help the poor. Her parents had never heard of him, but her mother liked that he was a priest and her father liked that he was a leftist. But they neither approved nor disapproved of her volunteering. They agreed that she should get to know Father Francisco and make her own decision about him. They only cautioned her not to divert too much time from her studies.

A few days later she got a phone call from Father Francisco, and they arranged to meet in Flores on a Friday, when she didn't have classes. He would take a *colectivo* from the *villa miseria* in Bajo Flores and meet her at a stop where he would get off, and then they would go together on a *colectivo* in the other direction, back to the *villa*. He said he didn't want her to try to go there by herself because it wouldn't be easy the first time for her to find the church in the maze of streets. So she was standing at the designated stop when he got off the brightly colored *colectivo*, waving to her and smiling at her.

"That worked," he told her. "So we're off to a good start."

"Yeah," she said with a good feeling.

They crossed the street and waited for a *colectivo* going in the other direction. She had things she wanted to ask him, but she didn't want to talk about them in public, so they made small talk until their *colectivo* arrived.

They didn't talk in the crowded bus, which she could tell was traveling from better to worse streets all the way to the end of the line. They were in a group of people who mostly had faces with brown skin and indigenous features, heading across the street to the *villa*. When they entered they were greeted by a complex smell of garbage, smoke, and human waste. The street wasn't paved, and there were almost no cars. A few boys were riding bicycles, and an old man was seated atop a wooden cart, drawn by a donkey. A stray dog tagged along with them, maybe hoping they would lead him to food.

They passed a variety of houses, including some of wood and other salvaged materials but mostly of brick, occasionally plastered over. Most of the houses were one story, with roofs of corrugated metal, but some of the houses were stacked as high as three stories, with roofs out of sight. In random places there were blue canvas sheets, presumably to keep out the rain and the cold at least until they could be replaced with more permanent materials. There were poles with improvised wires connecting to the houses.

Catalina had learned from her father that the *villa* didn't have an infrastructure for sewage and water, so the former mostly went into the ground and the latter was drawn from a river on its outer edge, which was badly polluted. Yet the children, especially the young ones, had scrubbed faces and clean clothes.

As they passed a family Catalina heard a language she didn't recognize, and Father Francisco told her it was Guaraní, which indicated that they were from northeastern Argentina or Paraguay or southwestern Brazil.

"Are most of them immigrants?" Catalina asked.

"Some of them are immigrants, but most of them are from Argentina."

Except for regular trips to Rio Cuarto and occasional trips to the nearby *campo*, Catalina had never been out of Buenos Aires, and it made her realize how little she knew about her country, which stretched from Antarctica to the tropics.

Having found a bag of garbage on the street, the stray dog had stopped tagging along with them by the time they reached the church, which had white plastered walls and an arch over the entrance with a brown wooden cross on top. They stopped, and Father Francisco said: "This is it. La Iglesia de Cristo Libertador."

"It's nice," she said, humbled by its simplicity.

He opened the door and led her into a space that was larger than she had expected. There were rows of benches, a simple altar, a crucifix on the wall behind it, and paintings on the walls to the left and right that depicted angels and saints.

"We offer Masses here twice a day," he told her, "early in the morning and early in the evening."

"Are they well attended?"

"Oh, yes. For most of these people it's the only positive thing in their lives."

She followed him into a side room which evidently served as his office as well as the sacristy, and he invited her to sit down in a folding chair in front of a desk, behind which he also sat down. After scanning her face he said: "Well, I know you have questions, so fire away."

She hesitated, not wanting to offend a priest, but she finally said: "I heard that you preach and practice liberation theology. Is that true?"

He smiled. "Yes. And you want to know what that's about?"

"Yes, I do. Could you explain it?"

"The simplest explanation is that it's putting into practice the teachings of Jesus about social justice. We consider Jesus not only as the redeemer but also as the liberator of the oppressed. Which explains the name of this church," he added for her edification.

She got it. "Okay."

"If you turn around and look at the wall behind you," he said, gesturing toward it, "you'll see in essence what liberation theology is about."

She turned and read the words that were written in calligraphy on the otherwise bare white wall: "The Spirit of the Lord is upon me, because he has anointed me to bring good news to the poor. He has sent me to proclaim liberty to captives and recovery of sight to the blind, and to set the oppressed free."

"It's from Luke 4:18."

"So it's about helping the poor," she said, feeling a connection with something deep inside her.

"Right. It's about the preferential option for the poor. And it's not a new idea. In fact, it runs through both the Old and New Testaments."

"Does it have anything to do with Marxism?"

He smiled understandingly. "I thought that was coming, *viste?* And the answer is, it has one thing in common with Marxism—the desire for social justice. But that's all. We don't believe that class struggle, which is inevitably violent, is a right way of achieving our goal. We believe in building society from the bottom up through the power of love."

"So what about the Montoneros?"

"What about them?"

"Well, I heard their leaders came from your Young Catholic Students."

He nodded sadly. "Yes, they did. I did everything in my power to stop them from resorting to violence. But they lost patience, and they lost the way."

"Then you don't support what they're doing?"

"No. I strongly condemn it. As I said at the meeting, violence is never justified, no matter how worthy your goal."

"Okay," she said, satisfied.

"Do you have any more questions?"

"Yes. I have one more question. How can I help you in your mission?"

His eyes lit up with a happy smile. "Well, here's how. You're at medical school with the intention of becoming a doctor—"

She waited for him to continue.

"How far along are you?"

"I'm in my fifth year, the last year of courses."

"So by now you know almost everything you can learn from going to school."

"I guess. Next year I'll do a residency in a hospital."

"That's fine" he said, "but you can also do a residency here."

"Do you have a hospital here?"

"No. But we have a clinic."

By now she had more than an inkling of why he had come to the medical school to recruit volunteers. "Where is it?"

"I'll show you. I'll introduce you to our doctor, who's here today. Come on," he said, getting up from his chair.

On their way to the clinic he told her a little about the doctor. Her name was Mercedes Saavedra, and she had a practice as a pediatrician in Almagro, a neighborhood to the east of Flores, closer to the city center. She had two adult children, a son and a daughter. The son was a cancer researcher, and the daughter was a high school teacher. She had raised them herself from the time when her husband was killed by the police in a demonstration against the military government of General Aramburu.

The clinic was a building about the same size as the church, with white plastered walls and windows protected by Spanish-style grates. Catalina followed Father Francisco into the clinic, where they were greeted by a woman with features similar to most of the people on the streets of the *villa*. She welcomed Father Francisco with affection.

Father Francisco introduced Catalina as a new volunteer for the clinic. The woman, whose name was Nevena, left them and returned with the doctor, a solid woman in a blue dress with light brown skin, prominent cheekbones, and deep dark eyes. The priest greeted her with an *abrazo*, and then he introduced Catalina to her, chatted for a while, and left them.

"Come on," Dr. Saavedra said, indicating the way to her office.

Catalina followed her and sat in a chair in front of a desk, as she had with the priest, repeating the scene but in a different context. She was glad that the doctor was a woman, who could provide a role model that she was lacking because the doctors who treated her family and taught her at the university were all men.

"So you're in your fifth year of medical school," Dr. Saavedra said, appraising her with those deep dark eyes. "Are you doing well there?"

"I'm getting good grades."

"Why do you want to be a doctor?"

"To help people," she said, repeating the answer she always gave to this question.

"Well, there are a lot of ways you can help people. So why this way?"

She paused to think. "I guess because it's a physical way of helping people."

"You mean as opposed to a mental way."

"Yeah, like helping people as a teacher or a therapist. Of course as a doctor I could help people in those ways too, but mainly in a physical way."

The doctor nodded as if she was satisfied with those answers. "Where do you live?"

"In Flores with my parents."

"Do they approve of your working here?"

"They don't know about you. They only know about Father Francisco. But they'll like the idea of my working in a clinic."

"It'll give you experience."

"That's what I want," Catalina said. "I want experience in the real world."

"Well, this is as real as the world gets," Dr. Saavedra assured her. "Which days are you free to work here?"

"Fridays are good. I don't have classes."

"What about Saturdays?"

"They're good too."

"So let's do Fridays and Saturdays. Those are the days when I need you most. I'm here on Tuesdays and Fridays, I have a resident from a hospital on Saturdays, and I have a nurse here every day, including Sundays. Nevena is a nurse."

"I thought she might be. Where's she from?"

"Her family's from Paraguay. She grew up in this *villa*, and she worked her way through nursing school. So she's a role model for the young women." The doctor paused. "In case you're wondering, I'm from Salta."

Salta was a province in the northwest of the country, bordering on Chile, Bolivia, and Paraguay. "I *was* wondering. You don't talk like you're from Buenos Aires. You talk like one of my professors who's from Galicia."

The doctor laughed. "That's interesting. My grandfather's from Galicia, so I'm a *gallega*, but my grandmother's indigenous, so I'm also a *mataca*."

"When did you come to Buenos Aires?"

"Thirty years ago. When I was fifteen my mother died, and my father went off the deep end. I had to fend for myself, and I didn't see any future in Salta, so I came here with no particular goal other than to have a better life. I supported myself by cleaning houses and working as a nanny. I lived in a poor neighborhood. It wasn't a *villa*, but it was poor. And one of the families I worked for decided to take a chance on me. They sent me to high school, and they helped me get into medical school. *Y aquí estoy yo.*"

"How long have you had the clinic here?"

"For six years. I was recruited by Father Francisco," the doctor recalled with a fond smile. "He was an assistant pastor at our church in Almagro, and he brought me here. We complement each other. I treat bodies, and he treats souls."

With a good feeling Catalina said: "Well, I'm glad he brought me here, Dr. Saavedra."

"You can call me Mercedes. I'll see you next Friday."

She stopped at the church to say goodbye to Father Francisco, but he wasn't there. A girl who was cleaning the benches said he was making a house call. So after kneeling and thanking God for Father Francisco and Dr. Saavedra, she found her way through the maze of streets back to where she had disembarked from the *colectivo*, and riding home, she knew she had found her mission in life.

THREE

OLIVIA HAD WANTED to join the mission of Father Francisco but her parents didn't want her to because they were afraid it would get her into trouble, and she had to respect their position. Anyway, Olivia and Catalina still commuted together to the medical school Monday through Thursday, and they still helped each other in their courses, so the divergence in their missions didn't affect their friendship. And Catalina shared her experiences in the *villa* with Olivia, who was always a good sounding board.

She had started work on the Friday following her introduction to Mercedes, and their first patient was a little girl about four years old whose mother said she had stomach cramps and diarrhea. Mercedes asked the mother how long the girl had displayed those symptoms, and if she was eating normally, and if there were signs of blood in her stools. It didn't take Mercedes long to diagnose the problem as intestinal parasites, probably giardia, which a lot of people in the *villa* had from drinking contaminated water from the river. Because this ailment was so common, Mercedes had in her refrigerator an effective medication which in liquid form was easier than pills for children to swallow. She gave a dose of the medication to the girl, and handed the mother a small plastic container of it, instructing her on how to use it and asking her to bring the girl back in three days. She also told her to boil all water before drinking it.

In medical school Catalina had acquired some knowledge of parasitical diseases, but this was her first experience in applying that knowledge, and as she observed Mercedes treating patients through the rest of the day she had a variety of experiences in applying knowledge, ranging from the treatment of young men for injuries from accidents or fights to the treatment of old women for chronic conditions from disease or lack of health care. By the end of the day Mercedes was confirmed in Catalina's heart as her role model, not only as a doctor but also as a woman.

Exhausted but feeling good about her first day at the clinic, Catalina decided to stop at the church to let Father Francisco know how much she liked her role in his mission. She arrived there as the evening Mass was about to begin, and she managed to find a place at the end of a bench in the rear of the church, which was filled with people. There was no procession, no entrance hymn: at the ringing of a bell a boy in an alb entered from the sacristy followed by Father Francisco. The boy was about her age, and he was cute. With his curly blond hair and pure blue eyes, he looked like an angel.

Along with the congregation Catalina made the sign of the cross and then participated in the penitential act and the other introductory rites. Since it was Lent there was no Gloria, and after the Collect the boy stepped to the lectern and did the first reading. With clarity and sensitivity the boy recited the poetry of Isaiah, including the lines: "No longer shall the sound of weeping be heard there, or the sound of crying. No longer shall there be an infant who lives but a few days, or an old man who does not round out his full lifetime."

That was followed by the psalm, which he sang unaccompanied in a soft tenor: "Sing praises to the Lord, O his saints, and give thanks to his holy name. For his anger is but for a moment, and his favor is for a lifetime. Weeping may last for the night, but joy comes with the morning."

The people responded, singing: "I will praise you, Lord, for you have rescued me."

The Gospel, which Father Francisco read very slowly, was about the royal official who asked Jesus to heal his son, who was near death. And just at the time when Jesus said "Your son will live" the fever left him, and he recovered.

Stepping out from behind the lectern and approaching the

people, Father Francisco gave a homily about the power of faith. It was plain and simple, using the language of the people and making the Gospel relevant to their own lives. He ended by encouraging them to have faith, no matter what happened.

Later, Catalina was impressed watching the people line up for communion. From their faces and their body language she could tell that they were deeply religious. She got into line behind them in the left aisle, and as she moved forward she noticed that the boy who looked like an angel was serving as an extraordinary minister as well as a lector and a cantor. She bowed her head to avoid seeing his face as she received the host from him, hearing him say: "The body of Christ."

"Amen," she murmured, turning away. She put the host into her mouth and made the sign of the cross as she headed back down the aisle, filled with something in addition to the usual feeling when she took communion which she couldn't identify. She guessed it might have come from being in church with deeply religious people, but she wasn't sure.

When the Mass ended she lingered, hoping to have a moment with Father Francisco, but he was fully occupied by people around him, with the boy at his side, and she didn't want to intrude on them, so she left the church and headed home.

Lying in bed that night she reflected on the events of the day, and the last image in her mind before she fell asleep was the boy who looked like an angel.

The next day she left home a little early so she would have time to stop at the church on her way to the clinic. The door to the office was open, so she leaned in and found Father Francisco sitting at his desk with papers in front him.

"I hope this isn't a bad time," she said, hesitating.

"No, not at all," he said, looking happy to see her. "In fact, it's a perfect time. I hate doing paperwork. *Pasa y siéntate.*"

"I won't stay long." She went in and sat down in the chair in front of his desk.

"I saw you at Mass yesterday evening. How did you like it?"

"I liked it a lot. I could tell how much it does for these people."

"I hope it does something for them. At least I get positive feedback from them, which wasn't always the case."

"It wasn't?"

"I celebrated my first Mass after ordination at a church in Barrio Norte, and when I told them in my homily that it was their duty to help the poor, they didn't like it. They asked the bishop to reassign me, which he promptly did."

Catalina had occasionally gone shopping on Avenida Santa Fe, so she knew that Barrio Norte was a neighborhood of rich people. "I'm glad he reassigned you."

"But he didn't reassign me here. He reassigned me to a church in Almagro, and he told me not to get involved in politics."

"Well, I don't see how helping the poor has anything to do with politics."

"It shouldn't, but it does. Unfortunately, it has everything to do with politics."

She thought about it, and then she said: "My father has a mission to help the poor. And he's a politician, a deputy in Congress on the left wing of the Peronist party."

"God bless him. But I think the left wing is losing out to the right wing."

"Yeah, that's what my father says. My grandfather, who was a communist, always said that Perón was a fascist."

"From what I see happening now, I think your grandfather was right." The priest paused, studying her. "Do your parents approve of your working here?"

"Oh, yeah. Their only reservation is that it might interfere with my studies."

"So don't let it. How many days will you work here?"

"Two. On Fridays and Saturdays."

"That's enough. Mercedes has two other students from the medical school plus a guy who's doing his residency at a hospital. So she has things covered."

Seeing an opportunity to ask a question about the boy who had done the readings and sung the psalm last evening, she asked: "Do you have students helping you?"

"Yes, I have three. You saw one of them at the Mass yesterday evening."

"He read very well, and he sang very well. Is he a seminarian?"

"He's in the social work program at the university. He's trying to decide whether to be a priest or a social worker."

"Do you think he'd make a good priest?"

"I think he would. But I think he'd also make a good social worker, so I'm not going to influence him either way."

"What's his name?" she dared to ask.

"Lucio. He lives with his parents in Caballito. They're good people. They came to the church in Almagro where I'm officially assigned so they could meet me."

She stopped asking questions, feeling she had gone as far as she could with the subject.

"If you want to meet him," the priest said with a twinkle in his eyes, "he'll be at our meeting tonight. We have a meeting on Saturdays after the Mass."

"At what time?"

"Around six. The Mass is at four on Saturdays. And after the Mass we get together, all the people who volunteer at the church, the clinic, and the school."

"There's a school?"

"Of course. It's not a public school, but it's open to everyone for grades one through five. It was started by the Sisters of Mercy, and it's staffed mostly by students in the education program at the university."

"Doing a residency?"

He smiled. "Yes. We have students in medicine, social work, and education. We also have a guy from the business program at Catholic University."

"What does he do?"

"He helps our businesses—the stores that sell food, clothing, and household items."

Impressed by the breadth of his program, she asked: "How many students do you have here?"

"About thirty. They're here on different days, so you don't see them all at once. They come and go, but there's a hard core of about fifteen."

"So where's the meeting?"

"At the school, which is on the same street as the clinic."

"Okay," she said, hoping that Lucio would be at the meeting.

They had a busy day at the clinic. Mercedes wasn't there but a guy who was doing a residency in orthopedics was there. His name was Orlando, and he was in charge. Among their patients was an old woman with a bad cough, a teenage girl who thought she might be pregnant, and a man who had broken his arm falling off a scaffold. They gave an antibiotic to the old woman to make sure that the cough didn't develop into something worse, they tested the girl and found that she was indeed pregnant, and they put a sling on the man's arm and sent him in a taxi to the nearest hospital, where they could do an X-ray and properly set the broken bone. Orlando was especially helpful with the man, explaining the procedures at the hospital, and Nevena, who had a lot of experience with pregnant teenagers, was especially helpful with the girl, counseling her and telling her how to take care of herself for the sake of the baby.

It was after six when they finally closed the clinic for the day, and Orlando walked with Catalina to the school. On the way they chatted about the professors they both had at the medical school and about their reasons for working in the *villa*. It turned out that Orlando was from San Isidro, a wealthy northern suburb, and it had been his father's idea for him to work at the *villa*, believing it would be good for him. Orlando said it was the best experience he ever had because it made him realize how blessed he was, and it made him feel good to share his blessings with people who were less fortunate.

They were late for the meeting, but it didn't seem to have started yet. Catalina estimated that there were about twenty people in the classroom who were mostly around her age. They were sitting in chairs used by an elementary school, at oblong tables where children did their daily work, so it wasn't ideal for a meeting.

Father Francisco presided, sitting on the edge of the teacher's desk, and when he spotted Catalina he introduced her to the group as the newest resident at the clinic. They welcomed her warmly with clapping and cheering.

Father Francisco began the meeting with a prayer, and then he called on the leaders of each group of volunteers to report on their activities. A nun reported on the school, Orlando on the clinic, Lucio on the church, and finally a tall, attractive guy reported on his efforts to help businesses in the *villa*. His name was Gastón, and from the way he presented himself it was obvious that he had leadership aspirations.

The meeting ended after less than an hour, but most of the attendees hung around. Being new, Catalina didn't know anyone except Orlando, and she was standing awkwardly by herself when the boy who looked like an angel came over to her.

"Hi," he said brightly. "I'm Lucio. You're Catalina, right?"

"Right. I work at the clinic," she added, feeling rattled and not knowing what else to say.

"I know," he said, revealing that he had asked Father Francisco about her. "You're a medical student."

"Yeah, I am."

"I'm in the social work program, but I help Father Francisco at the church. *Che,* didn't I see you at the Mass last evening?"

"Yeah, you did. I received the host from you."

"So that's where I saw you. I didn't recognize you, and I wondered who you were." He gazed at her with those pure blue eyes as if he had never seen anyone like her.

Something inside her responded to him, something she had never felt before.

"Where do you live?" he asked after a silence.

"I live in Flores."

"How do you get here?"

"By *colectivo.*"

"I live in Caballito, and I take a *colectivo* to Flores, where I change lines. So maybe we could go together as far as Flores."

"Okay," she said, welcoming his company.

A CONTRITE HEART

Sitting at the rear of the *colectivo*, where they had some privacy, they exchanged information about each other. She learned that he was the youngest of four children, all of them boys, and that he had been a late arrival, coming ten years after his next youngest brother. His father owned a store that sold appliances and provided services in plumbing and heating, and his mother was a teacher in an elementary school. His mother was descended from Irish immigrants who came to Argentina in the last century to work on the railroad being built by the British, and Lucio had inherited his blond hair and blue eyes from her side of the family. From the way he talked about his mother Catalina could tell he was close to her.

They reached her stop before they had covered the past and the present, and they hadn't begun to approach the future, so they still had a lot to talk about. And that night, as she lay in bed, she imagined conversations with him.

For the next six weeks she rode with him to Flores on the *colectivo*, and she got to know him within the limits of the time they had together. Then he proposed that they meet on a Sunday afternoon and go to a movie and have dinner at a restaurant, and she accepted.

Catalina had never gone out on a date before. She had gone out with girlfriends and with groups that included boys, but never alone with a boy. With the demands of medical school and the duties to her family she didn't have much time for boys. And before Lucio she had never met a boy she really liked. She had liked Lucio from the moment she first saw him serving Father Francisco in church, and her feeling for him had developed over the past six weeks to the point where she was almost in love with him. What held her back was knowing he might become a priest, and she didn't want to lose her heart to someone she could never have.

Of course as she was fixing her hair and checking her dress in preparation for her date, her brother Marco teased her about going on a date. Marco was only three years younger, but at times he acted ten years younger, and ever since she started medical school they had only a minimal relationship. He was in his second year at the university, studying law, but most of the time he seemed more interested in *fútbol* than in his courses.

Leaving the house she walked to the subway, where she got a train to the city center, and then she walked to Calle Lavalle, where she met Lucio in front of a movie theater. They were going to see *Chinatown*, an American movie starring Jack Nicholson and Faye Dunaway. Most of the movies she had seen were American, which usually didn't come to Argentina until long after they were released. During the last military government certain American movies were banned, and that made people want to see them.

Lucio was standing in front of the theater, and his eyes lit up when he spotted her.

"I have tickets," he told her. "So we can go in."

"Okay," she said, following him.

The tickets gave them reserved seats, which an usher led them to. It wasn't long before a big girl came down the aisle yelling: "*Helados, bonbones, caramelos.*"

"Would you like something?" he asked.

"No, thanks. I'm fine."

After the news, the ads, and the previews the feature began, and as she watched it she was conscious of being next to Lucio. In the dark theater it was more intimate than being next to him on a *colectivo*. She enjoyed the movie, and she enjoyed being next to him. And maybe he had the same feeling because he lingered in his seat until the last credits were gone from the screen and the lights went on.

Outside, it was dusk, and the street was thronged with people.

"Would you like to have dinner at a *parrilla*?" he asked.

"Yeah, that would be fine."

He led her down the street to a place that had a grill in front, with pieces of meat roasting over a fire. A waiter led them to a table for two, and after they had ordered a half carafe of red wine and some meat from the grill, he asked: "Did you like the movie?"

"Yeah, I did. I especially liked Jack Nicholson."

"He was great, and so was she. And it was a story that could have happened in Argentina."

"Yeah, it could have," she agreed. "I guess there's corruption everywhere."

After a pensive silence Lucio said: "You know, I want to make the world a better place. And that's what the detective in the movie was trying to do."

"Yeah, he was."

"So why did he fail?"

"He was up against something bigger than him."

"But aren't we always up against something bigger than us?"

"We are," she said, "if we're trying to change the world. But if we're trying to change only a part of the world, then I think we have a better chance."

"You mean like the *villa*," he said, reaching for a piece of bread.

"Yeah, we're making things better there."

The waiter brought the half carafe of wine and poured it into each of their glasses.

Lucio took a sip of wine and then said: "I don't know if Father Francisco told you, but I'm trying to decide whether I should be a priest or a social worker."

"He did tell me."

"The thing is, I have to decide which vocation would enable me to do more good for people. So what do you think?"

Not wanting to influence him, she said: "I think you could do as much good in both vocations."

"You do?"

"Yeah."

"When I'm with Father, I feel I should be a priest. But when I'm with you," he said, gazing softly into her eyes, "I feel I should be a social worker."

The implication wasn't lost on her.

"My mother," he said, "went to a Catholic school that was run by the Sisters of Mercy, *viste*? She loved the sisters, and she was going to become a nun."

"Why didn't she?"

"She met my father."

"So maybe you should ask your mother if she made the right decision."

"Yeah. Though of course she'll say she made the right decision. If she'd become a nun, I wouldn't exist."

She could have pointed out that if he became a priest his own potential children wouldn't exist, but she guessed that his mind had already gone there.

When the waiter brought their food they stopped talking while they devoured *asado de tira* and *papas fritas*, and when they were finished she had a feeling that a balance had been tipped within him, a feeling confirmed by the kiss he gave her at the entrance of the subway.

From then on they saw each other more often, including most Sunday afternoons. They didn't always go into the city center. At times they met in coffee shops in Flores or Caballito. They talked a lot. They talked about their families, they talked about their work, and they talked about their hopes for the future. She told her parents about her relationship with him, but she postponed introducing him to them until after the end of the semester. She would have two weeks of vacation then, so that would be a good time.

Meanwhile, as Catalina learned from daily conversations from her father, the situation in Argentina was deteriorating further. The president was letting López Rega, whom people called *El Brujo* (the Warlock), do anything he wanted, and the military were only waiting for things to get so bad that the public would welcome them back to the government. In June they forced out López Rega, and they replaced the commander in chief of the army who supported the government with a general who according to the rumors was ready to perform a coup. But they did nothing to stop the violence, and during the final weeks of the semester it got even worse, with more attacks by the Montoneros and more assassinations by the Triple A. In fact, without López Rega the Triple A was acting like a crazy monster with its head cut off, flailing around in every direction, blindly wreaking havoc on leftists.

At the end of the semester Catalina did well on her exams, and now she had only one more semester of courses to complete before she did her residency. During her two weeks of vacation she started the process of applying for a resident position in several hospitals, and she continued working two days a week at the clinic in the *villa*.

On a Friday morning when she arrived at the clinic she saw a sign on the door, saying: "*Solo emergencias.*"

Perplexed, she went in, and she found Mercedes sitting with Nevena in the waiting area. Nevena was sobbing, and Mercedes was comforting her, with an arm around her.

"*Qué pasó?*" Catalina asked with a spasm of fear.

"They killed Father," Mercedes said with tears in her eyes.

"What?" She couldn't believe it.

"He had just finished celebrating Mass at our church in Almagro, and a guy was outside waiting for him with a machine gun. The guy riddled him with bullets."

"Oh, my God." She crossed herself. And then as it hit her she burst into sobs, crying: "Oh, my God. Oh, my God."

Mercedes came to her and enfolded her in an *abrazo*, saying: "*No te desesperes. El padre Francisco está ahora en los brazos de Jesús.*"

After a while she managed to ask: "What are we going to do without him?"

"We're going to carry on."

She didn't see how, but she accepted the doctor's faith. And she went out and took the sign off the door that said they were only accepting emergencies.

For an hour there were no patients, which gave Catalina an eerie feeling. It was as if the people in the *villa* had disappeared, though she knew they hadn't because she had seen people on the streets on her way to the clinic. Thinking back, she seemed to recall that there weren't so many people as usual, and she wondered if the news about Father Francisco's death had gone around. And if people were hiding, she didn't blame them.

Around ten she asked Mercedes for permission to go and see what was happening at the church. She knew that Lucio usually got there around this time, and she was concerned about him. As she walked there she noticed that the few people she passed on the streets had grim faces.

When she entered the church it was empty, so she went to the office, and there she found Lucio sitting in a chair in front of Father Francisco's desk as if he had come there for a meeting. Tears were streaming down his cheeks.

Her heart went out to him, and she knelt down on the floor next to the chair, taking one of his limp hands and putting an arm around his waist and laying her head against his chest and saying: "I know, I know, I know."

For a long time they remained in that position, their bodies in a union of grief, and then he finally murmured: "Why did they kill him?"

"I don't know. I guess they felt threatened by him."

"But he would never hurt anyone. He always helped people."

"He always did. But for some reason they didn't like what he was doing."

"How could they not like it? Why would they even care about what he was doing?"

"I can't imagine. I can only assume that they have a different purpose in life."

After a silence he turned and faced her, asking: "How can we have a church without him?"

"We can't replace Father Francisco. But maybe we can find a priest who will come here and celebrate Mass."

"What priest would come here after what they did to him?"

"A priest who isn't on their list."

He looked doubtful. "Well, I could ask my mother to find a priest. She has a lot of connections in the church."

Standing, they embraced and held each other. Then she said: "You should go home now."

"Yeah," he said. "Until we find a priest there's nothing for me to do here."

She walked with him to the *colectivo* stop, and in parting she gave him a long, loving kiss with the hope that it would comfort him.

Back at the clinic, she wasn't busy because there were so few patients, and Mercedes told her she could leave early. On the *colectivo* she thought about Father Francisco, and overwhelmed by a feeling of loss, she couldn't help crying. The woman next to her asked if she was all right, and she only nodded while her tears kept flowing. Without a word, the woman gently touched her shoulder as if she understood.

FOUR

ARRIVING HOME SHE was glad to find her mother in the kitchen. Her mother still worked at her father's office, serving his political career as well as his legal practice, but now she had her own secretary, so her hours were more flexible.

Her mother turned from the stove and greeted her, asking: "What's wrong?"

Though she wanted to act like a grown-up, Catalina went into her mother's arms and cried like a child, incoherently telling her mother what had happened. And her mother comforted her, rubbing her back and assuring her:: "*Está bien, está bien.*"

When she finally sat down in a kitchen chair she asked: "Why did they kill him?"

"Because he was a leftist," her mother said.

"But he was a priest. And he was doing what the church teaches us. He was helping the poor. He was doing so much for the people in the *villa*."

"I know he was, but in their minds he was only a leftist. They didn't care if he was a priest. In fact, he's not the first priest they killed, and he won't be the last."

"But that's horrible. How can it be happening in our country?"

"Maybe it's our fate," her mother said, staring into the distance. "Maybe we're being punished for something we did."

"You mean that God is punishing us?"

"No. We're punishing ourselves. And we've been doing it for three hundred years."

After reflecting Catalina said: "Well, if they're killing leftists, then they could kill Dad."

"Of course they could. That's why I want him to resign from the Congress and concentrate on his legal practice. The Congress has no power anyway. The military have all the power, and it won't be long before they just do away with the Congress and stop pretending."

"But Dad has a mission."

"His mission is doomed. The military have no interest in helping the workers or the poor. They serve the rich, and they serve themselves."

"So is Dad going to resign from the Congress?"

"I've advised him to, and I hope he does."

"Well, whatever he does," Catalina said after a silence, "I'm going to carry on at the *villa*, at least until the end of the spring semester. By then I should have a residency at a hospital, but in the meantime Mercedes needs me at the clinic."

"You have our blessing, but be careful. Don't do anything that gets the attention of the military."

"I won't," she said, but she was committed to attending the funeral of Father Francisco and participating in actions to honor his memory.

That evening her father confirmed what her mother had said. According to his sources, the Triple A killed Father Francisco because he was a leftist. Her father also admitted that the military had all the power now, even though they weren't officially running the government, but he still had hopes that they would allow another election, in which he would run as a member of a new consolidated socialist party. And he assured Catalina that he wasn't in any more danger than a man on the street.

The next day around noon she went to the church and found Lucio there. He had good news. His mother had found a priest for them. The priest had other duties, so he could only do the Saturday afternoon Mass, but he said he might be able to get another priest to do one or two daily Masses. He was a missionary priest from Ireland, and the best news was that he had served for a while in northern Argentina, where he had learned not only Spanish but also Guaraní.

At four o'clock that afternoon Catalina was sitting on a bench near the front of the church when Lucio entered from the sacristy followed by a man in his early forties. He had light brown hair, a rosy face, and friendly brown eyes that scanned the congregation as if he was looking for people he knew. He had a northern accent, which appealed to the congregation, virtually none of whom were *porteños*, and in his homily he used a few words of Guaraní. All things considered, he did the best job anyone could have done following Father Francisco.

After the Mass, along with people outside the church, Catalina welcomed the new priest, whom Lucio introduced as Father O'Hara. She thanked him for the Mass, and after hearing about his missionary group she told him she hoped he could get another priest to come to the *villa*. Then, while Lucio accompanied him to the *colectivo* stop, she headed for the school, where Orlando had said they would have their usual meeting.

She wasn't surprised when she saw Gastón at the front of the room taking the leadership position, acting like the person in charge and greeting people by name as they entered the room. He began the meeting with a prayer, and then before calling on people to report on their areas, he talked about how he had met Father Francisco, about how Father had changed his life, and about his commitment to Father's mission of helping the poor. He then conducted the meeting formally as if they were in a business environment, which Catalina thought was just what they needed to hold things together.

When they had concluded the meeting Gastón told them where and when the funeral would be, encouraged them all to be there, and ended with a prayer. Catalina thanked him and joined Lucio for the trip home.

The funeral was held three days later at the church in Almagro where Father Francisco was officially assigned. The Mass was celebrated by the pastor of the church, and it was attended by volunteers from the *villa* and people Catalina didn't know but assumed were students or former students of Father Francisco as well as members of his family. She sat with Lucio in a pew near the front of the church, and they followed the Mass, they took communion, and they held hands during the final commendation. Sobbing, they watched the casket being wheeled down the aisle toward the entrance of the church.

On a bus that Gastón had hired for the purpose they rode to the burial at Chacarita Cemetery with other volunteers from the *villa*. They were mostly silent, weighted with grief. They stood around the graveside for the rite of committal, which included the words inscribed on the wall of Father Francisco's office: "The Spirit of the Lord is upon me, because he has anointed me to bring good news to the poor. He has sent me to proclaim liberty to captives and recovery of sight to the blind, and to set the oppressed free."

"*Gracias a Dios*," Catalina said along with the others.

They all held hands while the rite concluded with the Lord's Prayer and a final blessing from the priest. As she and Lucio walked out of the cemetery with their arms around each other's waist, she prayed for the courage to carry on.

She did carry on, completing the courses of her last semester with good grades and getting a residency at a good hospital. Since her residency began in March she had the summer off, and working at the *villa* five days a week she developed an even closer relationship with Mercedes, who had become her primary role model. Looking ahead, she envisioned her own life as a pediatrician and a volunteer at the *villa*.

By now she was tightly bonded with Lucio. Their mutual loss of Father Francisco was a turning point that made both realize how much they needed each other, and Catalina couldn't imagine a life without him. They saw each other almost every day in the *villa*, and they almost always did something together on Sunday afternoons. They went to movies, or they took walks, or they hung out at coffee shops. They talked about the future, and they talked about getting married, which they agreed would happen as soon as they were launched on their careers so that they could afford to rent an apartment and live together.

Meanwhile, things were going well at the *villa*. Father O'Hara continued doing the Saturday afternoon Mass, and he had found a priest who could do a Mass three days a week. Being off for the summer, Lucio had more time to help at the church and also to provide services as a social worker. Orlando was still working at the clinic on Saturdays, but he expected to be licensed as a physician by the end of the summer, so he was already looking for a regular position at a clinic in a working-class neighborhood, and since Catalina would be a resident at a hospital by then, she would replace him here. Another nun was teaching at the school, which didn't take the summer off, and Gastón had found a student at Catholic University to help him with businesses in the *villa*, which gave him more time for his leadership functions. Though he lacked the charisma of Father Francisco, he was doing a good job of holding things together.

For her residency at the hospital Catalina was assigned to a mentor, a pediatrician whose name was David Rosenberg. She met with him at the beginning of March, and she liked him immediately. He was in his early forties, with a kindly face and intelligent eyes behind silver-rimmed glasses. For their initial meeting, instead of sitting behind a desk, he pulled up a chair and sat beside her and began with questions about her family background. When she told him that her father was a deputy in Congress, representing the left wing of the Peronist party, he looked pleased. And when she told him that she was a volunteer at a clinic in a *villa miseria*, he looked even more pleased.

"That's the purpose of our profession," he said. "It's to serve people, not to make money."

"That's what my parents taught me," she said.

"So how many days a week are you working at the *villa*?"

"During the summer I was working there five days a week, but now I'll work there two days a week, if that's all right with you."

"It's definitely all right with me. Who's the physician you work with there?"

"Mercedes Saavedra."

His eyes lit up. "Really? I went to medical school with her. I haven't kept up with her, but I always hear good things about her."

"She's a good doctor and a good person."

"Well, since you've already done a residency, you know what's involved. For a while you'll just go around with me and observe what I do and ask questions."

A CONTRITE HEART

"I understand."

"The most important thing is to ask questions. If we ever stop asking questions," he said, "we stop learning. So do you have any questions about your residency?"

She paused for a moment. "I don't have any questions now, but I'm sure I will later."

"Then I'll see you here on Monday. Take care."

She was struck by the way he said "Take care" as if he really meant it. He wasn't just saying it. And she left his office with a good feeling.

Three weeks later a military junta overthrew Isabel Perón. They arrested her during the night and took her away in a helicopter. By early morning they had blocked all radio and television stations, replacing their content with military marches. After a while they broadcasted their first communiqué, which said: "People are advised that as of today the country is under the operational control of the Joint Chiefs General of the Armed Forces. We recommend to all inhabitants strict compliance with the provisions and directives emanating from the military, security, or police authorities, and to be extremely careful to avoid individual or group actions and attitudes that may require drastic intervention from the operating personnel."

The members of the junta, General Jorge Videla, Admiral Emilio Massera, and General Orlando Agosti, were all extreme rightists. Their program, which they euphemistically called the National Reorganization Process, was to root out leftists from all institutions in Argentina. They implemented a state of siege in which unionists, journalists, and political activists were abducted from their homes and their workplaces, and even on the streets. It was clear from the efficient execution of their program that they had spent the last several months preparing to take over.

Of course they dissolved Congress, which left Catalina's father without an official position. Her mother expressed relief because she thought he would no longer be a target of the military, though her father wasn't so sure about that. To placate her mother, he switched his focus to his legal practice and promised to stay out of politics, though he still received information from unofficial sources that didn't make him happy.

One evening he sat down with Catalina in the living room and shared his concerns with her, beginning with the statement: "In the past when the military took over they at least talked about having elections. But this junta isn't even talking about elections, which suggests that they'll be in power for a while."

"For how long?" she asked.

"For as long as it takes to eliminate all vestiges of Marxism."

"Do you think they'll come after you?"

"I don't know. They're going after everyone, so they might come after me."

She didn't have to ask him about the implications.

"So if anything happens to me," he told her, "I want you to have a fallback. As you know, we have family in New York. It's a cousin whose father immigrated to America at the same time my father immigrated to Argentina."

She had heard about this cousin, whose name was Angelo.

"Their fathers made a bet. My cousin's father bet he would do better in America, and my father bet he would do better in Argentina. Well, based on the situation now, it looks like my cousin's father won that bet."

"Not necessarily," she said, wanting to be positive.

"Now, maybe nothing will happen to me, but if it does I want you to go to New York."

"What about Mom and Marco?"

"They won't be targets," her father assured her. "And they can go to Rio Cuarto, where the military won't bother them."

"But you think they'll bother me?"

"They might. They could connect you with Father Francisco, and of course they're against what you do in the *villa*."

"They are? Why?"

"They think it's promoting Marxism."

"Marxism? But the church teaches us to help the poor."

"Whatever it teaches, it supports the military."

"How can it teach us to help the poor and at the same time support the military?"

"Because the church doesn't like Marxists any more than the military do."

"Well, *my* church isn't that way."

"*Your* church isn't the establishment. *Your* church has a mission to help the poor, so it's out of favor with the establishment."

Catalina reflected. "I hope you're not saying I should stop working at the *villa*."

"No. I support what you're doing. You and I have the same mission. But I'm telling you that if anything happens to me I want you to go to New York." Her father paused. "I wrote to my cousin, and he said he'd give you a safe haven. He's an artist, so he doesn't have a lot of money, but he said he'd have room for you in his apartment."

"Okay," she said. "But nothing's going to happen to you."

"You never know," her father said grimly.

The next day he started the process of getting her a passport, and since he still had bureaucratic connections it only took a month for her to get it. He told her to have that document with her, along with her *cédula*, at all times.

She got off to a good start at her residency. She liked the hospital, she liked the nurses, she liked the staff, and she really liked Dr. Rosenberg. He was such a good doctor, such a good teacher, and such a good person. She felt blessed to have been assigned to him. But one morning, after she had worked with him for about three months, she went to the hospital and didn't find him there. She asked one of the nurses on their floor where the doctor was, and the nurse said she didn't know, but she thought he might have an emergency at home with one of his children. Accepting this explanation, Catalina did her job as well as she could without her mentor for the rest of the morning. By noon, with the doctor still missing, she asked the floor manager where the doctor was, and the manager said she didn't know. In fact, the manager had called personnel to see if they knew where the doctor was, and they didn't know. And that made Catalina worry because she didn't think Dr. Rosenberg would not call and let them know if for any reason he couldn't come to work.

By the late afternoon, with the doctor still missing, she heard rumors about the possibility that he had been arrested. She didn't want to believe these rumors, but not having any other explanation she couldn't dismiss them, so during a break she asked a nurse about them.

The nurse, who was about her mother's age, was reluctant to talk about the rumors, but she said it was possible that Dr. Rosenberg had been arrested,

"Why do you think it's possible?" Catalina asked.

"Because he's a Jew," the nurse said.

"So?" Catalina didn't understand.

"So he could be a Marxist."

"A Marxist?"

"Yeah. Marx was a Jew, so in their minds any Jew could be a Marxist."

"But that's ridiculous," she said. "It's guilt by association."

"I know it is, but it's how they think. So you should be careful what you say."

Not wanting the nurse to be found guilty by association with a leftist resident, Catalina immediately ended the conversation and went back to work.

At home that evening she asked her father if the government was arresting Jews. He said they were, and he explained that the military had a long tradition of anti-Semitism. The previous military government had arrested Jews who were writers, journalists, actors, musicians, and professors, and during that period a number of Jews went into exile. Her father confirmed what the nurse had said about the military equating Jews and Marxists, so he said it was possible that Dr. Rosenberg had been arrested.

The next morning she found Dr. Rosenberg in his office, looking terrible. He asked her to sit down, and he said: "I'm sorry. I'm really sorry."

Not understanding, she waited in silence for him to explain.

"You're doing so well," he told her, "and I know you'll be an excellent pediatrician. But I can't mentor you any longer."

Assuming it was because of her leftist associations, Catalina didn't ask him why.

But then he said: "I'm leaving Argentina. I'm taking my family to New York."

She had learned that he had two children, a girl who was twelve and a boy who was ten.

"I can't stay here after what happened."

"What happened?" she asked him.

He took a long breath and let it out slowly. "They came to my home the night before last, and they arrested me. They didn't tell me why, but I could guess, especially after they questioned me. They kept asking me about my connections with Marxists, over and over. They didn't torture me, but they kept me up all night."

"I'm sorry," she said, feeling for him.

"I don't care what they do to me, but I have to think about my wife and my children."

"I understand."

"I did my residency at New York University Hospital," he said. "I called them yesterday, and they said there was a very good possibility of their having a position for me. Of course I'd have to get recertified, but they said it would help that I did my residency at that hospital."

"So when would you leave?"

"As soon as possible. When they released me, they told me I was on their list."

"Do your children speak English?"

"They studied it in school, and they're young enough to learn it fast. And my wife speaks English. So we won't have a language problem."

"That's good." She tried to imagine what it would be like for a twelve-year-old girl to change countries, to go from winter in Argentina to summer in America.

"As for your situation, I've asked personnel to assign you to another mentor. They're working on it. And meanwhile you can carry on as you did in my absence. The nurses said you did a great job," he added, smiling.

"Thanks," she said, appreciating it.

"I'm really sorry that I won't be able to mentor you through your residency, but I hope you understand."

"I do. And I'm glad I got to work with you at least for a while. I've learned so much from you. I mean, you've been a great mentor."

He extended his hand to her, saying: "I hope we'll see each other in the future, maybe in New York."

"Yeah, maybe," she said, shaking his hand.

Two days later in a meeting with the head of personnel she was told that she no longer had a position at the hospital, and she was advised to look elsewhere. She wasn't given any explanation.

That evening, when she told her father what had happened he gave her an explanation: she was on their list. And he advised her to think about going to New York. She did think about it, lying awake in bed that night, but she didn't want to leave her family, her boyfriend, and her country, so she decided to stay and deal with the situation.

The next morning she told Mercedes what had happened, and Mercedes agreed with her father, saying: "You're on their list. We're all on their list. And that worries me, but it would worry me more if I wasn't on their list."

Catalina understood. "So should I look for a position at another hospital?"

"Yes, you should. But I'll talk with the university, and I'll try to get them to let you fulfill the residency requirement by working with me."

"You think they'd do that?"

"I don't know, but it's worth a try. I mean, you'd get as much experience working here as you'd get at a hospital."

"Okay," she said. "And in the meantime I'll look for a position at another hospital."

Over the next few weeks she went to every hospital in the

metropolitan area, and she applied for a position. The people she talked with were noncommittal, so she couldn't tell what her chances were, but at least she had a fallback at the clinic.

Meanwhile, the military intervened the university, attacking programs that they believed were most likely to harbor Marxists. A prime target was the social work program, which was effectively closed for Lucio by the cancellation of courses that he needed to complete his degree. So he was understandably despondent, seeing himself without a career.

They talked about his situation in the church office late one afternoon on a day when there wasn't a Mass. She tried to cheer him up, pointing out that they were both in the same situation, and he said: "Yeah, but at least you got to complete your courses."

He was one year behind her even though he was two years older because he had spent time in a seminary before beginning the social work program. "But until I complete a residency I can't be licensed as a doctor."

"You said they might accept your work with Mercedes."

"They might, but they haven't made a decision yet. And now that the military have intervened the university, they probably won't accept it."

"If they don't, then we're both fucked."

Teasing him, she said: "If you were a priest you wouldn't talk like that."

"If I was a priest," he said, "I wouldn't be in this position."

"I hope you don't regret it," she said, feeling responsible for his decision not to be a priest because if he hadn't met her, he might have been a priest.

"No, I don't," he said resolutely. "I still believe that I can do more good for people being a social worker, if only they'll let me be one."

"Well, my father says that the military will be in power for a long time, but not forever. He says they always reach a point where things are going so bad for them that they decide to hand the government over to civilians."

"How long was the last military government in power?"

After counting she said: "About seven years."

"That's a long time."

"It is," she admitted. It was one third of the whole time she had been alive.

"I don't see how I can wait that long."

"You don't have to wait. You can do things in the meantime."

"What can I do?"

"You can do what you're doing now," she told him, "what I'm doing, what we're all doing. You can carry on."

Encouraged, Lucio carried on, and he kept finding new ways of doing good for the people in the *villa*, counseling them and helping them to improve their lives. Catalina knew how well he was doing his job because she had him accompany her on house calls when the only problem wasn't physical. Often the problem was mental, and there were addictions to alcohol and drugs. She would never forget a particular time when she was treating a woman for wounds inflicted by her husband who had flown into a drunken rage against her. Lucio took the man aside, and instead of blaming him tried to get him to understand the anger within him and learn to manage it. And as far as she knew the man stopped taking it out on his wife.

By the end of June she hadn't procured a residency at another hospital, and she hadn't heard from the university that they would accept her work at the clinic as fulfillment of the residency requirement, so she and Lucio were basically in the same situation of having their careers stalled by the military. But they were both fully committed to their work at the *villa* as an end in itself, and believing that their situation wouldn't last forever, they dealt with it. The only problem was that neither of them had a paying job, so they still had to live at home with their families, a common situation for people their age.

They worked at the *villa* through the long winter while the military tightened their grip on the country. The government launched an economic plan that Catalina didn't understand, but her father explained that it was based on theories of the Chicago school of economics, according to which you could grow the economy by giving incentives to the rich, and the rising tide would lift all boats. But in reality, her father said, it would lift only the boats of the rich. And as the months passed, the economic plan wasn't helping the country in ways that she could understand. There were still very high rates of inflation, unemployment, and poverty.

Around the middle of October, while a welcome spring was underway, she read in the newspaper that the Montoneros had bombed a military club in Buenos Aires. She understood that the Montoneros had committed this atrocity to retaliate against the military for its ruthless campaign to exterminate them, and it wasn't the first time the Montoneros had attacked the military. But she could see that bombing the club was especially outrageous because it not only killed a number of officers but it also showed the public how vulnerable the military were, having been attacked at an inner sanctum.

In the days that followed the bombing the military redoubled their efforts to rid the country of the Montoneros and of everyone who sympathized with them. And though it didn't come as a total surprise when Catalina arrived at the *villa* one morning and found that the church, the clinic, and the school had been bombed during the night, it was still a shock. Except for the rubble of bricks and cement and metal and glass there was nothing left of what Father Francisco had built for his mission.

FIVE

STANDING BY THE remains of the clinic, Catalina learned from a man who had joined them that no one in the *villa* had been hurt by the explosions because the buildings were free standing, at a distance from the nearest houses, and the attack occurred in the middle of the night when no one was around.

She was imagining what might have happened if the bombs had exploded during the day with patients in the clinic or children in the school or people in the church when she spotted Gastón coming their way. They exchanged greetings, and then he joined them in a moment of silence after which he said: "We're going to have a meeting. You know the café near the *colectivo* stop? We're gathering there at eleven o'clock. So please join us."

"Okay," she said automatically.

When he had left them Mercedes said: "I hope he doesn't want to rebuild the church and the clinic and the school."

"You do? Why?"

"Whatever we rebuild here, they'll only destroy it. They don't like what we're doing here."

"I know they don't like it, but I hope you're not saying we should stop doing it."

"No, I'm only saying we shouldn't have buildings for them to bomb. We can serve these people without buildings."

"Well, I can see how the clinic could serve them without a building. We could make house calls. But how could the church and the school serve them without buildings?"

"The church could have prayer groups, and the school could have study groups. They could meet in houses and in stores. It wouldn't be ideal, but it could work."

"So maybe that's what Gastón has in mind."

Mercedes shook her head. "I don't think so. He's ambitious,

and he wants to do big things. But in this situation, with the military watching us, we shouldn't do big things, we should settle for doing little things."

"You mean things that don't attract their attention."

"Right. It's the way of St. Therese."

Catalina understood because St. Therese of Lisieux, with her little way, had been a role model during elementary school. "So I'll suggest that at the meeting. Will you be there?"

"I'll be there if you want moral support."

"I do," she said, not only wanting it but needing it.

Concerned about Lucio, she went to the church and found him standing by its remains. He looked so lost that her heart went out to him, and she gave him a long, comforting hug.

"Why did they do this?" he asked her.

"I don't know," she told him, "but I think they did it to retaliate for the bombing of the military club."

"But we didn't do that. The Montoneros did it."

"They don't distinguish between us and the Montoneros. Remember, the leaders of the Montoneros were members of the student group that Father Francisco mentored, so in their minds all his followers are Montoneros."

"So we're guilty by association?"

"In their minds we are. I mean, look what they did to Dr. Rosenberg because he's a Jew."

"Well, I can't imagine what goes on in their minds."

"I can't either," she said, taking his hand.

For a long time they gazed in silence at the rubble, and then he said: "So how are we going to rebuild the church?"

"Mercedes thinks we shouldn't rebuild it."

"She does? Why not?"

"She thinks they'll destroy it."

"What about the clinic and the school?"

"She thinks they'll destroy whatever we rebuild."

"But how are we going to pursue our mission without a church, a clinic, or a school?"

"By leading prayer groups, making house calls, and having study groups."

"I could do my social work by making house calls, but how could people receive communion without a church?"

"The priests could also make house calls. It's how they give communion to people who are homebound."

"Well, I guess they could."

"Are you going to the meeting?"

"Yeah. Are you?"

"Oh, yeah," she said. "I'm going to suggest how we can carry on. And Mercedes will be there to support me."

"I'll be there to support you," he said, putting an arm around her shoulder.

Shortly before eleven they walked to the *colectivo* stop and over to the café, where about fifteen people were gathered in the back, standing around as if they were waiting for instructions. Gastón and a boy who taught at the school were moving tables so they could sit together, and when he was ready he said: "*Bueno.* Let's begin the meeting."

Catalina sat with Lucio and Mercedes while the others sat in groups according to their area of work. A few arrived late, so there were about twenty people by the time Gastón, standing at the head table, bowed his head and said a prayer.

Then he raised his head and said: "We all know what happened last night. We know who did it, and we know why they did it. But I don't think we should let them stop us from pursuing our mission. Do you agree?"

There were murmurs of assent.

"So the only question is how we should proceed. I think we should rebuild the church and the clinic and the school. What do you think?"

"Where would we get the money?" a girl asked.

"Don't worry about the money. I can raise it. I want to know if you agree that we should rebuild the church and the clinic and the school."

Catalina raised her hand.

"Yes, Catalina?"

"I think we shouldn't rebuild them, at least not now. If we do, they'll only destroy them."

"You think we should be afraid of them?"

"I don't think we should be afraid of them. I think we should respect their power and work around it."

"How would we do that?" Gastón asked her. "How would we serve the people here without a church, a clinic, or a school?"

"We don't need buildings. Speaking for the clinic, we could make house calls. The church could have prayer groups, and the school could have study groups."

"Where would they meet?"

"In houses and stores."

Gastón frowned. "There wouldn't be room for many people in houses and stores."

"The groups would be small," she said, "and that might even work better. Instead of having twenty kids in a classroom, we'd have five or six."

"But what about the church? You couldn't have Mass in small groups. We don't have enough priests for that."

"The priests could make house calls to give communion."

Looking around, Gastón said: "I don't see any priests here. Are you speaking for them?"

"No, I'm not. I'm only making a suggestion. But isn't that what Father Francisco did before he built the church?" She had no idea what he did, but she took a chance that no else at the meeting knew, including Gastón.

"Well, thanks for the suggestion, Catalina. Does anyone want to comment on it?"

"Yeah," Lucio said. "I support the suggestion. It's the right way to pursue our mission, and it would work."

"Thank you, Lucio. Anyone else?"

"I support the suggestion," Mercedes said. "It would not only work, but it would also be sustainable. It wouldn't attract attention from the military because there wouldn't be anything for them to see. But if we rebuild the church and the clinic and the school, they'll see them, and they'll destroy them. And next time we might not be so lucky. Next time they might hurt people."

"Thank you, Dr. Saavedra. Anyone else?"

No one else commented.

"Are there any other suggestions?" Gastón asked.

There were no other suggestions.

"So let's have a vote," he said. "How many people want to rebuild the church and the clinic and the school?"

A few hands went up.

"And how many people want to follow Catalina's suggestion?"

All but a few hands went up, including the hand of a nun who taught at the school.

"Then we'll follow Catalina's suggestion," Gastón said stolidly. "I'm asking each area to prepare a plan, with a schedule of house calls, prayer groups, and study groups. Lucio, you can do the plan for the church. Catalina, you can do the plan for the clinic. And Inés, you can do the plan for the school. We'll meet here on Saturday at six o'clock."

As she walked out of the café Catalina felt good, especially about how Gastón was following her suggestion, even though it wasn't his idea, and she gave him credit for accepting the will of the majority.

Though they had decided to provide services to the villa without buildings they still needed a base of operations with storage space, a bathroom, and a place to hang out, at the very least. They solved this program by fixing up an abandoned house, which took a few weeks, and it turned out that they could use it for prayer groups and study groups. They could also use it for a communications center where people in need of medical services could send a child or a neighbor and request a house call. The main challenge was in scheduling the use of the house, for which Gastón assumed responsibility.

He was doing a good job, but Catalina could tell that he wasn't happy, so she wasn't surprised when a few weeks later he told her that he was leaving to undertake another project. He had found a *villa miseria* to the west of the city, out near the Ezeiza Airport, and his project was to build a church, a clinic, and a school there. Since that *villa* had no connection with Father Francisco and was probably well beyond the range of the military's surveillance, he believed that he could escape their notice and pursue his mission there without interference. Catalina thought it was a good idea, and if she hadn't been committed to her mission in this *villa* she might have been tempted to join Gastón at the other *villa* because she respected his leadership abilities.

Of course she had to take over his responsibility for scheduling the use of the house, which put her in a leadership position, but she discovered that she liked it, and she learned to allocate her time between providing medical services and administering the mission. She was gratified when other volunteers, including Mercedes, told her she was doing a very good job, and she shared her feeling with her parents, who as usual gave her their full support.

In early November the jacarandas, which signaled the arrival of spring, were blooming and raising her spirits as always when she was awakened in the middle of the night by a pounding on the front door. She sat up in bed, and she heard her father go downstairs, and then she heard a man yelling, ordering her father to do something. She put on her bathrobe and went out to the hall, where she saw her father heading to her parents' bedroom.

Pausing, he said: "Don't go downstairs."

"What's happening?" she asked him, suddenly afraid.

"They're taking me away, and there's nothing you can do to stop them, so don't try."

"Who is it? The police?"

"They say they're police, but I don't believe it. I think they're military."

A voice from downstairs yelled: "Come on! We're waiting."

Her father went into her parents' bedroom, and after only a few minutes he came out, dressed, followed by her mother.

Pausing again, her father quietly told her mother: "Don't go downstairs. Call Gustavo and tell him they're taking me away. He'll know what to do."

"I'll pray for you," her mother said, hugging him.

Catalina watched her father go downstairs, and she couldn't

stop herself from creeping down to the landing to see what was happening.

There were two men with guns, and seeing her, one of them pointed his gun at her and said: "Go back upstairs, or I'll kill you."

She lingered long enough to see the other man steer her father out the front door, and then she retreated back upstairs. She found her mother in the bedroom, talking on the phone. She waited, trying to follow the conversation. When her mother finally hung up, she asked: "Were you talking with Mr. Bianchi?"

"Yes. He's going to talk with the police and try to find out what's happening."

"Dad said he didn't think it was the police. He thought it was the military."

"Mr. Bianchi will find out if it was the military," her mother said with confidence.

"If it was," she asked, "what will they do to him?"

"They'll question him. They'll want to know if he's involved in antigovernment activities, and since he's not involved in any such activities, they should let him go."

"They let Dr. Rosenberg go after questioning him, and they didn't hurt him physically."

"Well, they have no reason to hurt your father. He never hurt anyone."

Since they had no chance of getting more sleep, they got dressed and went downstairs to the kitchen without disturbing Marco, who had slept through all the commotion. Her mother made coffee, which they drank while waiting for Mr. Bianchi to call back. Catalina knew that Mr. Bianchi had served as a legal counsel to her father's wing of the Peronist party, so he had connections and knew how things worked.

Though they were expecting it, they both jumped when the phone rang.

Catalina listened to her mother's end of the conversation, which was mainly limited to: "Yes. Yes. Yes, I see."

When her mother hung up she stared ahead with a look of deadly fear in her eyes.

"What did he say?" Catalina asked her.

"He said it *was* the military," her mother said in a flat voice. "The police don't know where they took your father."

"Will Mr. Bianchi try to find out?"

"Oh, yes. He knows someone in the military. But he said we should—" At this point her mother choked on the words. "—we should be prepared for anything."

She didn't have to ask what that meant. She went to her mother and hugged her, trying to comfort her as much as she was being comforted. She prayed that they wouldn't hurt her father, and that they wouldn't hold him long.

Catalina stayed home with her mother that day, waiting to hear from Mr. Bianchi. Her brother eventually got up, and when her mother told him what had happened to his father he didn't seem to understand. He just kept asking stupid questions.

By noon her mother got another phone call from Mr. Bianchi, who said he would come over to their house in about an hour. Believing that what he had found out was something he could only tell them in person, Catalina was scared. And she prayed again, and again, and again that the military wouldn't hurt her father.

Mr. Bianchi arrived in less than an hour. He was a short man with hair only around his head, sad dark eyes, and a drooping mustache. He followed Catalina and her mother into the living room, where he sat down in the chair where her father usually sat.

"I'm sorry I kept you waiting," he said, addressing her mother. "I understand how hard it is not knowing what happened to a loved one."

Her mother only nodded, encouraging him to continue.

"I talked with my contact in the military, and he made inquiries about your husband. It took him a while but he finally learned that they took him to the ESMA."

"What's the ESMA?" her mother asked.

"The Escuela Superior de Mecánica de la Armada."

"The Naval Mechanics School?" Catalina said. "What happens there?"

Mr. Bianchi sighed. "What I'm going to tell you is strictly

confidential. If anyone asks me if I told you what happens there, I'll deny it."

If she was scared before, she was even more scared now.

Her mother only nodded.

"That's where they take people to interrogate them. It's not a good place."

She had to ask: "Do they torture people there?"

"I hear they do, though not always."

"So sometimes," she said, "they torture people, and sometimes they don't?"

"Well, that's what I hear, but I don't know."

"Do they ever release people from there?" her mother asked in a quavering voice.

"Sometimes they do," Mr. Bianchi said.

"But sometimes they don't?" Catalina asked him.

Again he sighed. "Sometimes they don't. But I started a process to have him released."

"What kind of process?"

"A legal process."

"Do they respect the law?"

"Sometimes they do."

"So you might not be able to have him released."

"I might not. I only have the law, which they only respect if it suits them."

"Would it suit them to release a left-wing Peronist?"

"It might, but honestly I don't see how."

"In other words," her mother said, "there's not much hope that they'll release him."

"I'm sorry," Mr. Bianchi said, looking as if he really meant it. "There's not much hope. We can only pray for his release."

After three days of waiting Catalina finally went to the *villa*, and when she entered the house that was their base of operations she found Lucio sitting at her desk. He jumped up and came to her and hugged her, saying: "I'm so sorry."

"You heard what happened to my father?"

"Yeah. I heard on the news that the military arrested a Marxist traitor, and since he had your last name I guessed it was your father."

"We're still hoping that they'll release him, but we don't know."

"When will you know?"

"Well, our lawyer says if they don't release him within a few weeks, we should assume they won't release him."

"You mean they'll put him in prison?"

"They might, but from what our lawyer tells us, prison would be a blessing."

"Lord, have mercy," Lucio said.

"So how are things here?" she asked, changing the subject.

"They're fine," he said. "I've been doing your job, but not as well as you, so I'm glad your back. We have a new teacher."

"Really?" She was glad because they needed more teachers for the study groups.

They were still catching up on the administration of their mission when Gastón came into the office, and he looked at her as if he too had heard about her father. She told him what she had told Lucio, and then she asked him what he was up to.

He told them he was making progress. A friend, who was a real estate agent, had found a *quinta* that was for sale. Since people used *quintas* during the summer, and since the summer had already begun, his friend didn't expect to sell this *quinta* for a while, so it was available for Gastón to use, free of charge, and it was only a half mile from the *villa miseria* that he had selected for his mission. The *quinta* had five bedrooms, so in theory it could accommodate ten people. He had recruited six people, so there was room for Catalina and Lucio if they wanted to join him. She politely thanked him for the invitation, but there was no way she could leave her mother at this time. Gastón said he understood, but if things changed and if he still had an empty bedroom they could always join him.

Before leaving, he gave them directions on how to get to the *quinta*. He had a car, which he had driven here today, but there was a *colectivo* stop within walking distance. It was a long ride from the city center, but he had tried it before he bought the car, and it had given him time to relax and think about his project.

Catalina spent a sad Christmas with her mother and her brother. As usual they went to Mass at the Basilica San José de Flores, where she prayed for the safe release of her father, and as usual they had a roast chicken with potatoes and carrots for Christmas dinner, with a bottle of sparkling wine. But the holiday didn't raise their spirits.

After two months of hoping for good news and still not receiving any her mother confronted the stark fact that without any income from the law firm she couldn't afford to live in Buenos Aires, so she decided to move back to Rio Cuarto and work for her family's business, which her brother had taken over. She had talked with her brother, who said they could use her professional skills. And moving back to Rio Cuarto was what her husband had advised her to do if anything happened to him. So she closed the law firm and put the house up for sale.

Catalina had some long conversations with her mother, who wanted her to go to Rio Cuarto, but that would have meant leaving Lucio, so she resisted the idea. She even discussed with Lucio the possibility of his going with her to Rio Cuarto, and he said he would go anywhere in the world to be with her. But if they ever had the opportunity to complete their degrees they couldn't do that in Rio Cuarto, and in the meantime unless there was a *villa miseria* in Rio Cuarto they couldn't pursue their mission there. So she told her mother that if she could find a place to live she would stay in Buenos Aires.

Of course she had in mind the *quinta*, which two days later she and Lucio checked out after a long *colectivo* ride. The *quinta* had a traditional ranch house with white plastered walls and a terra cotta roof. In front was a lawn, with sheltering trees around it, and in back was a swimming pool. Inside was a large main room that served as a dining and living room, two full bathrooms, and five bedrooms, one of which was still unoccupied. It was more luxurious than the house where Catalina had lived her whole life, and she tried to imagine being rich enough to afford it as a summer place.

After Gastón showed them around she and Lucio wandered out across the lawn to the wall of trees through which they got a glimpse of the desolate immensity of the pampa.

"So what do you think?" she asked him.
"I think it's fine," he told her.
"I mean, do you think we're ready to live together?"
"I think we are. And if we're not, this will give us a chance to find out."

They sealed their decision with a long kiss.

The next day she met with Mercedes in the café outside the *villa* where they often had meetings. She told Mercedes about her mother's decision to move back to Rio Cuarto, and about her own decision to stay in Buenos Aires.

"The thing is," she said, "I need a place to live, so yesterday Lucio and I went to the *quinta* that Gastón is using."

"Where is this *quinta*?" Mercedes asked.

"It's out near Ezeiza. It's a long ride on a *colectivo*, but I won't be going back and forth. My work will be at the nearby *villa*."

"Is Lucio going with you?"

"Oh, yes. He's a main reason why I'm staying in Buenos Aires."

"A main reason?" Mercedes arched her eyebrows. "Are there are other reasons?"

"There's one other reason. I want to pursue my mission, and I don't know if I could do that in Rio Cuarto."

"They must have poverty there."

"I'm sure they do, but not like here."

After taking a sip of coffee Mercedes asked: "What about your father?"

"We haven't heard anything. And that's what makes it so hard," she said, struggling to hold back tears. "I mean not knowing what happened to him."

"They do that deliberately. It's supposed to discourage people from opposing them."

"My father opposed them, but he wasn't doing anything to them. He was only doing what my mother wanted, practicing law. So why did they take him?"

"Your father was a public figure. They knew his political views. And since he was a socialist, he was high on their list."

"So where are you and I on their list?"

"We're probably somewhere near the middle."

"And once you're on their list, you're always on it?"

Mercedes nodded. "You always are, unless they take you off it."

She didn't have to ask how they took you off it. Hopefully, she said: "Well, maybe we won't be so visible at that *villa*."

"You probably won't be, and now we're not so visible here without the church, the clinic, and the school. Unless they have a spy among us, they have no idea what we're doing."

"You think they'd have a spy here?"

"No, I don't think so. They made their point by bombing our buildings, and unless we do something that attracts their attention, they'll leave us alone."

"Well, I wish I could stay here with you, but I need a place to live, and I can pursue my mission there as well as here."

"You can," Mercedes said. "The only thing that concerns me is that Gastón plans to build a church, a clinic, and a school there. Which could get their attention."

"So I should get him to change his plan?"

"I think you should. If we can provide services here without buildings, you can do it there. And you know how."

Early in January her mother got an offer for the house, and it took several days to remove the furniture and personal things. Catalina helped her mother with the task, with desultory assistance from her brother. It was painful going through her father's books and papers, most of which they saved. They only threw out things that should have been thrown out long ago, but there was still a lot for the movers to pack into the van that was parked on the street in front of the house. As she stood on the sidewalk with her mother and Marco, watching the van drive away, Catalina had a feeling she would never see its contents again.

Later that day she went with her mother and Marco in a taxi to Aeroparque Jorge Newbery, and she accompanied them to the gate for the flight to Rio Cuarto. Waiting with them, she wondered if she had made the right decision to stay in Buenos Aires, and she was tempted to go with them. She was carrying a backpack with things she would need at the *quinta*, as well as the doctor's bag she had used in Bajo Flores, so all she had to do was buy a ticket and join them on the plane with her carry-on luggage.

She was held back by her feeling for Lucio, which completely overwhelmed her other feelings. She hugged her mother, she hugged Marco, and she watched them board the plane. She stood there for a long time after the plane had taken off. It had struck her that for the first time in her life she would be on her own. Her mother had given her some money, which would last for a while. With a free place to live she only had to pay for food, and she assumed that the group at the *quinta* would pool their resources for groceries. But after a while the money would run out, and she would have to find a job, not as a doctor but as an assistant to someone in a hospital. She could bear that comedown as long as she could pursue her mission.

She took a taxi from the airport to Plaza Miserere, where she got a *colectivo* for the first leg of her journey to the *quinta*. When she finally arrived there after transferring to another *colectivo* and walking the final half mile, she was welcomed by Gastón, who showed her the bedroom she would share with Lucio. With his sophistication Gastón probably assumed that she and Lucio were sleeping together, though in reality because they lived at home with their parents they hadn't gone beyond kissing. And what she imagined happening when they shared a bed would be another first time in her life.

Lucio wasn't there yet, and when he hadn't shown up by the late afternoon she began to worry that something had happened to him. Since he was on their list the military could have taken him for questioning. She tried to dismiss this possibility, but after what had happened to her father she couldn't make it go away. She racked her memory, making sure that they had agreed to meet at the *quinta* today. And though she imagined other things that might have delayed him, she still worried that the military had taken him for questioning.

When he finally walked into the main room, where they were all sitting at a round table, passing a bowl of pasta, she jumped up and hugged him for dear life.

"*Disculpá,*" he told her. "I missed my connection."

"She was worried about you," Gastón said. "But let me assure you, all of you, that the military don't know where we are or what we're doing."

"We're under their radar," a boy agreed.

"So have a seat and enjoy the meal. I hope you like pasta because we're going to live on it. At least until we have more money."

Lucio put his backpack aside and sat down in the chair next to her, putting an arm around her shoulder.

"I was worried," she told him. "We're on their list, and after what happened to my father—"

"I know." He kissed her softly on the neck.

"Hey, hey," Gastón said. "Not at the dinner table. And now that we're all here, I should introduce you. This is Lucio. I know him from the *villa* in Bajo Flores. He served at the church, and he helped people. He's a social worker."

"Not yet," Lucio said. "I still have a year of courses to complete."

"Welcome to the club," a girl said. "My name is Violeta, and I was studying to be a teacher."

The others introduced themselves, going around the table. They were all university students whose careers had been stalled by the military's interference with their programs. There were four of them in education, three in social work, one in medicine, and two in business. There were eight guys and two girls, including Catalina, who was glad she wasn't the only girl.

When the bowl of pasta finally came around to Catalina and Lucio, there wasn't much left, so Gastón got up and took it into the kitchen, and when he came back with the bowl refilled, Catalina took a big helping, which she devoured as if it was the last food she would ever see.

They sat around and talked until it was late. She noticed that Violeta was paired with a guy who was also a teacher, and after saying goodnight they headed for their room. She felt nervous as she watched the others go off to bed, and finally when she couldn't delay it any longer she got up and led Lucio to their room. She stood by while he unpacked his backpack and put his clothes into the drawers of the bureau that she had saved for him. She waited until he went off to the bathroom before she undressed and got into her nightgown, and when he returned she was lying in bed. She was amazed by how quickly he took off his clothes and joined her in bed, wearing only a tee shirt and shorts.

"Are you okay?" he asked her gently.

"Yeah, I'm okay," she told him.

Then he kissed her, and after that everything went as naturally as possible. Her last feeling before she fell asleep was that they were now bonded for life.

SIX

THE NEXT MORNING after breakfast of coffee and bread Catalina and Lucio walked to the *villa* with Violeta and the guy with whom she shared a bedroom, whose name was Ignacio. It took them about twenty minutes to get there, and on the way they shared backgrounds. Violeta was from a working-class neighborhood in the south of Buenos Aires where her father was the head of a local union. Ignacio was from Tandil, a city in the province of Buenos Aires, out on the pampa. He started his program at a branch of the university in Tandil and came to Buenos Aires to complete his degree. Like the others he was a follower of Father Francisco.

The *villa* resembled the one in Bajo Flores, though it was smaller and more of the people had brown skin with indigenous features. As they walked through the streets Catalina heard a number of people speaking Guaraní and another language that she didn't recognize. In the middle of the villa they stopped at a house that was evidently under construction.

"This is our base of operations," Violeta said. "At least until we get our money."

"What money?" Catalina asked her.

"The money that Gastón raised."

"Where's it coming from?"

"A nonprofit organization," Ignacio said. "They're funded by an American charity whose mission is to help the poor."

"An American charity? That's great." It reassured her to know that the expected money was coming from America, which had all the money in the world.

"When do we hope to get this money?" Lucio asked.

"Within a month," Violeta said. "It's all arranged. They just have to do some paperwork."

"As soon as we get our money," Ignacio said, "we can start building a school here."

"Who's going to build it?" Catalina asked.

"The people in the *villa*. We'll pay them for their work, so we'll create jobs."

"In the meantime," Violeta said, "we're providing services as you've been doing in Bajo Flores. Gastón told us how you do it there without a church, a clinic, or a school."

"Gastón managed our operation, and he was good at it."

"After he left," Lucio said, "Catalina managed our operation, and she was good at it."

"So would you like to manage our operation here?" Violeta asked her.

"I wouldn't mind, but only if Gastón wants me to."

"I think he does," Ignacio said. "He told us he was recruiting someone with management skills, and since you guys got the last bedroom, you must be it."

Catalina never would have described herself as someone with management skills, but Gastón must have described her that way because he was a business student.

The four of them spent the rest of the morning walking around the *villa* and talking with people. Watching and listening, Catalina was impressed by the number of people that Violeta and Ignacio knew, and by the relationships that they had developed. It gave her a very positive feeling, and she was glad she had joined the group.

Catalina needed medical instruments and supplies, so the next morning Gastón drove her into the city to buy them. On the way they talked, and she took advantage of the opportunity to learn more about him. She began by asking: "How did you meet Father Francisco?"

"He came to our university to talk with students," Gastón said. "He told us about his mission, and I was inspired by it. In fact, it changed my life."

"It did? How?"

"It made me realize that I didn't have to do what my father wanted me to do."

"What did your father want you to do?"

"He wanted me to take over his business. He owns a factory that makes refrigerators, and it was his idea for me to go to the university and study business."

"Did you have your own ideas?"

"No. Until I met Father Francisco, I got my ideas from my father. But after I heard Father Francisco talk about his mission, I realized that I didn't want to spend my life making refrigerators. I wanted to make the world a better place."

"Refrigerators are useful," she pointed out.

"They're not useful for people who don't have electricity. When Father Francisco took me to Bajo Flores and I saw how little those people had, I wanted to help them. I wanted to give them education, health care, and jobs."

"That's what my father wanted to give people."

"I'm sorry," he told her sincerely. "Have you heard anything about him?"

"No, I haven't. I can only hope and pray."

"I hate what the military are doing, *viste*? In fact, before I met Father Francisco I thought the solution was to overthrow them by violence. I knew some guys who joined the Montoneros, and I seriously thought about joining them. But after listening to Father Francisco I realized that there's a better way than violence. We can overthrow the military by building a just society from the bottom up, one *villa* at a time."

"We can," she agreed. "We should never resort to violence like the Montoneros. I just don't understand why they abandoned the principles they learned from Father Francisco."

"Well, I can understand their frustration," Gastón said. "When you run into a brick wall, you want to smash through it. But it's better to go around it."

"Yeah." She paused and then asked: "So what does your father think about what you're doing?"

"He doesn't like it. The last time I saw my father he said I should haul my ass back to the university and get my degree in business."

"Well, maybe someday he'll appreciate what you're doing."

"Maybe. I hope so."

She imagined what her father would think about what she was doing, and she was comforted by the belief that he would support it.

Now that she had medical instruments and supplies she was ready to go to work, and over the next few weeks she called on people at their houses. Most of them trusted her immediately, though a few of them had to be won over. As usual, most of the men didn't want to admit they had health problems, and some of the children were hard to communicate with because they only spoke Guaraní. But as soon as she developed a good relationship with the mother she was able to provide effective services because the mother was the heart of the family.

Meanwhile, Lucio was going around the *villa* getting to know the families and counseling them. In the process he was picking up words of Guaraní which he shared with her in the evenings after dinner, and the next time they went into the city to get supplies they bought a Spanish-Guaraní dictionary. They practiced Guaraní with each other, and soon she found that she was able to communicate better with the children.

Underlying her work was her relationship with Lucio, which was flourishing as a result of her being on her own, away from her family. Of course she missed her mother and even her brother, and she was still mourning the loss of her father, but being with Lucio, talking with him, sharing a bed with him, and making love with him more than compensated her for not being with her family. So on balance she was happy, and every morning and every evening in her prayers she thanked God for all her blessings.

One evening, as they were sitting around the table after dinner, Gastón made an announcement that changed everything: the military had intervened the nonprofit organization that they were counting on to provide money for their mission.

"They did?" Catalina asked him. "Why?"

Facundo, the other business student, said: "They claim this organization is supporting Marxist activities."

"Marxist activities? Since when is helping the poor a Marxist activity?"

"In their minds," Gastón said, "anything that doesn't help the rich is a Marxist activity."

"But the money is coming from America," Ignacio said.

"So? What's your point?"

"America supports the military."

"Their government supports the military, but their charities don't support it. They pursue their missions."

"So the military told this organization that they can't pursue their mission here?"

"Yeah, that's what they told them," Gastón said.

"How do you know?" Violeta asked.

"They told me. They said they were sorry, but they have to stop their operations in Argentina."

"So where does that leave us?" Catalina asked.

"It leaves us without a source of money."

"Could we get money from another nonprofit organization?"

Gastón shook his head. "If their mission is to help the poor, the military will intervene them. Let's face it, the military don't like what we're doing."

After a silence Catalina said: "If we can't raise money to build a church, a clinic, and a school, then we should continue pursuing our mission without those buildings."

"I would agree," Gastón said, "if there wasn't another way to raise money. But there *is* another way to raise money."

They waited for him to explain.

"We could raise money the way the Montoneros do it."

Catalina was shocked. "You mean kidnap someone and hold him for ransom?"

"It works for them, so it could work for us."

"But it's against what we believe in."

Gastón paused. "Do we believe in helping the poor?"

"Yeah, we do, but—"

"Do we believe in funding our mission with available sources?"

"Legitimate sources, but not—"

"Look. We had money coming from that organization, and the military took it away. So the military *owe* us that money."

"Yeah, they do," Facundo said.

"So if we take it back from them," Gastón argued, "why is that not a legitimate source?"

"Because kidnapping is *not* legitimate," Catalina said forcefully. "Kidnapping is an act of violence."

"It's only an act of violence if you hurt the person. If you let him go, it's only an exchange of money for his freedom."

"The Montoneros," Facundo pointed out, "have hardly ever hurt people they kidnapped."

"They did at least once," Lucio said.

"Yeah, but out of how many kidnappings?"

"The Montoneros have always gotten away with it," a teacher whose name was Sergio said.

"Well, we're not the Montoneros," Violeta said. "And what if we get caught?"

No one had to say what the military would do to them.

"We won't get caught," Gastón said. "The military won't come after us. They'll think the Montoneros did it, and they'll go after them. And we'll pick someone who won't generate much publicity. I mean, we don't want publicity, we only want money."

"Do you have someone in mind?" Sergio asked.

"No, I don't. Right now I just want to know what you think about the idea?"

"I think it's wrong," Catalina said.

"I do too," Lucio said.

"I think it's a great idea," Facundo said.

"Should we take a vote on it?" Gastón asked.

There were murmurs of assent.

"Before you vote," Catalina said, "I hope you understand that kidnapping is a major crime, and even if everything goes all right we'll be guilty of it."

"In the minds of the military," Gastón argued, "we're already guilty of a major crime."

"But what if something goes wrong?"

"Nothing will go wrong."

"It might if they do something unexpected."

"You mean the military? They don't do unexpected things."

"They're too dumb to do unexpected things," Facundo said.

"Don't underestimate them," Catalina said.

After a pause Gastón asked: "Are there other arguments for or against?"

Catalina didn't say anything more. She had a feeling that the vote would go against Gastón as it had in Bajo Flores, so she was surprised—in fact, she was shocked—when the group voted six to four in favor of the idea, with her and Lucio and Violeta and Ignacio voting against it.

That night in bed she and Lucio had a long conversation. They were both adamantly against the idea, but at the same time they felt solidarity with their friends. And if they didn't go along with them, they couldn't stay here at the *quinta*. They discussed the possibility of living with their families as they had before, but that would separate them, and by now they were used to living together. They also discussed the possibility of living together with one of their families, but they couldn't do that without getting married, and while they planned to get married in the future they weren't yet ready to get married. In any case, they felt that living with either of their families would be a step backward.

Last but not least, since they were against the use of kidnapping to raise money for their mission, they had a responsibility to stop it from happening, and if they left the *quinta* now they wouldn't be in a position to stop it, or at least to make sure that the victim of the kidnapping didn't get hurt. If they left now, and if the victim did get hurt, they would still feel responsible, and they would still be held accountable by the military. So they decided that staying and trying to stop the kidnapping was better than leaving and evading their responsibility.

Over the next few weeks Gastón and Facundo worked together to identify a target for the kidnapping. It had to be someone in the military, high enough in rank to have ransom value but not high enough to have tight protection. They decided that a colonel was the right level, and Gastón, with the help of a journalist friend who wasn't yet on the military's list, identified a colonel who was stationed in Buenos Aires. His name was Nicolás Yribarren, and he had presided over a massacre of Montoneros in Chaco Province. A group of Montoneros who had been captured and held in prison were being transported to another prison in military vehicles when an order was given to stop the convoy, and then according to the journalist the female prisoners were raped and some of the male prisoners were castrated, along with other tortures, before they were killed and buried in a nearby cemetery where graves had been prepared for them. The military reported that the convoy was attacked by Montoneros, and that some of the prisoners were killed in the shooting while the others escaped. But the journalist had a source for the true story, the most important element of which was that the order to stop the convoy and kill the prisoners was given by Colonel Yribarren.

After sharing this information with the group Gastón said: "He's a perfect target. The Montoneros have a motive for revenge against him, and the military know this, so when he gets kidnapped they'll think the Montoneros did it."

"He's an evil man," Facundo said, supporting the plot, "so he deserves to be kidnapped."

"But you wouldn't hurt him," Catalina said.

"We wouldn't hurt him," Gastón assured her. "But of course he won't know we wouldn't hurt him, so being kidnapped will make him suffer."

"I still don't like it," Catalina said. "No matter how bad a person he is, we shouldn't make him suffer."

"No, we shouldn't," Lucio said.

"Well, I don't like what he did to those prisoners," Gastón told them. "And kidnapping him is a much lesser evil than what he did to them."

"So how are we going to kidnap him?" Sergio asked.

"I haven't worked that out yet. We know where he's stationed, and we can follow him home from work to find out where he lives and what he does in his free time."

"If he's a colonel, he'll have a car with a driver."

"That's not a problem," Gastón said. "Facundo and I can follow him in my car."

"Is that your next step?"

"Yeah, that's our next step."

After the meeting Catalina and Lucio went to their room, where they discussed the situation. It was one thing when the kidnapping was only an idea, but it was another thing now that they had a prospective victim, and they could see that the more it became a detailed plan the harder it would be to stop. So they went back to the main room, where they met with Gastón and tried to convince him not to proceed. They used every argument they could think of, short of threatening to go to the police, which of course was out of the question because it would be suicidal. And when Gastón refused to back down, they finally had to settle for making sure that he didn't hurt the colonel.

It took Gastón a few weeks to work out the details. By following the colonel they learned that on Fridays he didn't go home after work but instead went to a restaurant to have dinner with a friend, and after dropping off the friend he went to a club called Minas, where men were entertained by bargirls. The plan was to have a bargirl at Minas who would lure him away to a hotel, where they would abduct him and bring him to the *quinta*. From his journalist friend Gastón had identified an appropriate hotel where you could rent rooms by the hour. The hotel wasn't far from the club, so it wouldn't take them long to get there. The girl would lead the colonel into the hotel, and the driver would wait for them. Facundo would follow them into the hotel, and after a while he would come out with a message for the driver telling him that he could go home and he wouldn't be needed until Monday morning because the colonel planned to spend the night there. Meanwhile, the girl would leave the door of their room unlocked, and before anything could happen between her and the colonel, Gastón and Facundo would rush into the room and chloroform the colonel, whom they would take down in the elevator and through the lobby, pretending that the colonel was drunk and that they were helping him. Outside, they would put him into the trunk of Gastón's car, and they would drive away. Since the colonel lived alone in an apartment no one would know he was missing until the driver went to pick him up on Monday morning.

After he had presented his plan Gastón invited questions from the group, asking if they could see any flaws.

"Won't the police be able to track the colonel to the hotel?" Sergio asked.

"The hotel doesn't keep records of its clients," Gastón said.

"What about the club?" Ignacio asked. "Won't they remember that the colonel was there?"

"The owner of the club and the people who work there don't want to get into trouble with the military, so they won't remember anything."

"Who will play the role of the girl?" Violeta asked.

That was the question Catalina was going to ask. With only two girls in the group, either she or Violeta would have to play the role of the bargirl.

"I haven't decided," Gastón said.

At the end of the meeting he asked Catalina to stay, and when everyone else had left the room he said: "I think you can guess what I have in mind for you."

"Yeah, I can guess," she told him, "but I won't do it."

"Just think about what we can do with the money. We can build a church, a clinic, and a school. We can do so much more to help those people."

"How much money are you going to ask for?"

"I'm going to ask for what they stopped the nonprofit from giving us."

"How much was that?"

"Three hundred thousand dollars."

"You think they'll pay that much for this colonel?"

"I know they will. Esso paid the Montoneros twelve million for one of their executives."

"Well, I know you think it's right to get the money they stopped us from getting, but I still think it's wrong to get it by kidnapping."

"You care about this *hijo de puta* who ordered his men to torture and kill those prisoners?"

"I condemn what he did, but it's not my place to judge him."

"It's not your place to judge him? It's not your place to judge the people who tortured and killed your father?"

"I don't know what they did to him."

"You know what they do to prisoners at the ESMA."

"I've heard what they do, but I still don't know what they did to my father. And whatever they did to him," she said, trying to hold her ground, "it's still not my place to judge them."

"If you don't judge them," Gastón said, "then you're letting them get away with murder."

"This isn't about them, it's about the guy you want to kidnap."

"Yeah, it is. It's about the guy who ordered his men to torture and kill more than twenty young people who were followers of Father Francisco. It's about the money that the military took from us. It's about justice."

"I understand," she said, unable to argue against these points. "But I still think it's wrong to kidnap someone."

"It's only wrong if we hurt him," Gastón maintained, "and we won't hurt him."

"How could I be sure that you wouldn't hurt him?"

"You could be sure that we wouldn't hurt him if you played a role in the kidnapping."

"I don't see how."

"I'll tell you how. This colonel will only get hurt if something goes wrong, and by playing a role in the kidnapping you can make sure that nothing goes wrong. If Violeta did it," he added, "something probably would go wrong."

"Well, I don't think Violeta would do it. She voted against the kidnapping."

"You're right. She did. And frankly I don't think she could lure this guy to a hotel."

Though she didn't like his disrespect for Violeta, she admitted to herself that he was right on this point. She couldn't imagine Violeta luring a guy to a hotel. "Well, if I did it, and I'm not saying I will, exactly what would I have to do?"

"You'd have to get a job at that club as a bargirl."

"A bargirl?" She grimaced.

"Don't worry. Bargirls don't sleep with clients unless they want to. Their job is to entertain clients and get them to buy bottles of champagne."

"How do they entertain clients?"

"By talking with them and by dancing with them."

"You seem to know a lot about this club."

"I scouted the place for two weeks."

"Then people who work there might remember you."

"As I said at the meeting," Gastón told her, "people who work there don't remember anything."

"Okay," she said. "But they might remember the bargirl who lured the colonel away."

"They might, but they won't remember you. They'll remember a girl with black hair."

"I don't have black hair."

"You'll wear a wig."

By now her resistance was being undermined by all the details that he had worked out. And from working with him she respected him. But she still didn't want to play a role in anything that could end up hurting a person, even a person as evil as the colonel. And she finally said: "Promise we won't hurt him."

"I promise we won't hurt him."

"Well, I have to talk with Lucio before I make any decision."

"I understand," Gastón said. "Take your time."

Lucio was against it. As they discussed it that night, lying on their bed, he gave her a long list of reasons why she shouldn't do it beginning with the fact that kidnapping was a major crime, as she herself had pointed out when Gastón first presented the idea. Yes, they were already on the military's list, but if they committed a major crime they would rise to a higher level on that list. And if they got caught for kidnapping an army colonel they didn't even want to think about what the military would do to them.

Catalina argued back that by playing a role in the kidnapping she could make sure that nothing went wrong, but if she didn't get involved then something could go wrong, and because of their association with Gastón the military would come after them anyway, even though they hadn't been involved in the kidnapping. So it would actually be less risky to get involved than not to. Accepting her arguments, Lucio agreed that she should do it though only after being assured that she wouldn't let a client touch her, including the colonel.

Over the next several days Gastón prepared her for the role. He bought a black dress that showed a bit of cleavage, he bought a black wig that made her look alluring, and he rehearsed her background story. Her name was Martina Aguirre, she had come to the city from Santiago del Estero, she lived alone in a studio apartment, and she worked at a shop in the jewelry district that didn't pay her enough to live on, so she needed extra money. She was available on Friday nights from opening to closing.

When she tried on the dress and put on the wig and looked at herself in the mirror, Catalina laughed, and so did Lucio, who joked that she looked like a hooker. All that was lacking was red lipstick and eye shadow, which Violeta helped her to apply. When she looked again at herself in the mirror she shuddered at the thought of what her mother would say.

The *quinta* had a telephone under the name of whoever had owned it back in the days when you could get a phone without knowing someone in the government, but Gastón wouldn't let anyone use it because a call from that phone could be traced to their location, so posing as a dealer in escorts he used a pay phone in the city to call the club and schedule an interview for Martina Aguirre. He told Catalina not to worry about the interview. If the owner of the club liked what he saw he wouldn't ask for references, and he wouldn't ask any personal questions. All he wanted was a girl who could lead on horny guys and get them to buy bottles of champagne.

The interview was even easier than Gastón said it would be. The owner was a tiny man with birdlike eyes and a birthmark on top of his bald head. From the way he ogled her, Catalina could tell that he liked what he saw, and after less than twenty minutes he offered her a job on Friday nights with hourly pay plus a bonus for the bottles of champagne that she got clients to buy. As she left the club she had mixed feelings, dreading what she would have to do but reminding herself that it was to raise money for their mission.

Gastón drove her into the city for her first night of work. The club was in an elegant French-style townhouse on a side street off Avenida Santa Fe, and it had a forbidding doorman who let her in after finding her name on his list of bargirls. Feeling out of place, she headed for the bar, where girls were hanging out. They greeted her, exchanged names, and continued chatting about things like shoes and clothes.

Eventually guys came into the club, in pairs or threesomes or foursomes, talking and laughing and raising the noise level to a point where the background music of recorded popular songs was barely audible.

A guy with regular features, pinkish white skin, and naive blue eyes approached her and asked: "Do you speak English?"

Catalina had studied English in school, though she hadn't used it very much, but since he didn't look like such a bad guy she said: "Yes, I do."

"Would you like to sit down and have a drink?"

"Okay," she said. She spotted a table and led him to it.

When they were seated he asked: "How do I get a drink in this place?"

"I can order for you. What would you like?"

"Oh, I don't know. I hear you have good wine in this country."

"We do," she said. "We have excellent champagne. Would you like a bottle?"

"Yeah, sure." He leaned back in his chair, relaxing.

She signaled the waiter, who went to get a bottle of champagne. Of course it was Argentine, which technically wasn't champagne, but not knowing the difference Catalina liked it when her family had it to celebrate the arrival of the New Year.

"I'm from Texas," the guy told her. "Houston, Texas. Where are you from?"

"I am from Santiago del Estero."

"Santiago del Estero?" he said, mispronouncing it. "What's that?"

"It is a province west and north of here."

"What happens there?"

"Oh, not much. That is why I am here in Buenos Aires."

He gazed across the table at her with baffled eyes. "You know, you don't look Spanish."

"I am not Spanish. I am Argentine," she told him proudly. "I am part Spanish and part Italian."

"Well, I'm American. I'm part English, part Irish, part German, and part something else."

At that point the waiter arrived with the bottle of champagne, which he set on the table in a bucket of ice. He carefully poured a glass for the American and a glass for her. According to her instructions she wasn't supposed to drink her champagne, she was only supposed to sip it and to get her client to keep drinking so he would order another bottle. As she watched him drink she wondered how old he was. If he was here on business, which seemed likely, he had to be at least thirty, but he didn't look it. In fact, he looked so young and innocent that she felt bad about taking his money for an overpriced bottle of champagne.

He started talking about himself, saying he worked for an oil engineering firm that had a contract with the Argentine national oil company. He even went into detail about his work, but then he must have noticed that she wasn't following him, so he changed the subject, asking: "How late do you work?"

"Until we close."

"What time is that?"

"It is usually around four in the morning."

"Four in the morning? When do people sleep here?"

She shrugged. "Whenever we can."

"Well, if I wanted to see you after work, how could I go about it?"

"You could stay until four," she told him, doubting that he would stay that long.

As if he intended to stay that long he asked her to order another bottle of champagne, which she promptly did. And she dutifully listened while he talked more about himself, telling her about the different countries he had traveled to, including Saudi Arabia, where they did business in ways that he would never understand.

He didn't stay until four. In fact, he didn't stay much past eleven, and he was staggering out of the club when she noticed a man in uniform come in. The insignia of a colonel, which Gastón had showed her a picture of, was on the man's shoulder, and his features, which Gastón had made her study a picture of, were those of Colonel Yribarren.

Her moment had come.

SEVEN

THE COLONEL, WALKING with deliberate steps, approached the bar where Catalina was hanging out with girls who were presently between clients. He was a tall man with tight lips, an aquiline nose, and cold gray eyes, which swept across the faces and bodies of the girls as if they were evaluating merchandise. When his eyes landed on her, Catalina smiled reflexively.

Stopping in front of her, he asked: "Are you free?"

"I am right now," she told him, implying that if he waited she might not be free.

"So get us a table," he ordered her.

She led him to a table and sat down across from him and asked: "Would you like a bottle of champagne?"

"Of course. That's what you're here to sell, right?"

Noting that he was more sophisticated than her American client, she signaled to the waiter to bring a bottle of champagne.

Meanwhile, he took off his hat and set it on the table, revealing a head of closely cropped dark hair. Examining her face, he said: "I don't remember seeing you here before."

"I'm new," she said. "I just started tonight."

"Well, it's good to have some fresh girls. Where are you from?"

"Santiago del Estero."

He smiled wryly. "I've been there, so I can understand why you left that dismal place and came to Buenos Aires. How long have you lived here?"

"Not long," she said, evading the need to invent details.

"You must have another job."

"I do. I work in a shop in the jewelry district."

"The jewelry district?" he said with distaste. "Is the owner of the shop a Jew?"

"No, I don't think so," she said. "He has a Spanish name."

A CONTRITE HEART

"That doesn't mean anything. They take Spanish names and hide behind them. I hope he doesn't treat you badly."

"He treats me all right."

"But he doesn't pay you enough to live on, which is why you're working here, right?"

"I do need extra money," she agreed.

At that point the waiter arrived with a bottle of champagne, which he poured into both of their glasses. While the colonel took a sip from his glass she watched the bubbles rising in her glass, reminding herself to be careful.

"Do you have a boyfriend in Santiago?"

"No. I don't."

"Do you have one here?"

"No," she lied.

"Well, that's good. Are you free after work?"

"I might be," she said, not wanting to make things too easy for him.

"I know you're supposed to stay here until closing time, but I don't think the owner would mind if you skipped out early."

"I'd have to ask him," she said, but she had no intention of asking him because she didn't want to draw attention to her departure with the colonel. When the time came she would have to pretend to ask the owner for permission to leave early.

He finished his glass of champagne and poured another, saying: "I know the girls aren't allowed to drink."

"We're allowed to drink a little but not too much."

"I wouldn't want you to drink too much." He scanned the upper part of her body, with his eyes pausing on her cleavage. "I hope you didn't go to a Catholic school."

"I didn't," she lied. "I went to a public school."

"That's good. I had a bad experience with a girl who worked here. She went to a Catholic school," he explained, "and she wouldn't do things I wanted her to do."

Swallowing, she said: "I'm open to anything you want to do."

He grinned. "Terrific. We'll have a great time together."

By now a live band was playing: a keyboard, a bass, and a singer, doing a repertoire of classic songs like "Bésame mucho."

Deciding it would be less risky to dance with him than to talk with him, Catalina invited him to dance with her, and he responded positively. They got up from the table and went to the floor where two or three couples were dancing.

Though Catalina didn't consider herself a good dancer, she recognized that the colonel was a good dancer, and she let him lead her within the confines of the small floor. Being close to him she smelled his cologne, which repelled her, but she put up with it, reminding herself of her mission. She became uncomfortable while the band played "Amor" and he pulled her closer, rubbing his pelvis against her and making her aware of his hard-on, which probed at her as if it was looking for the entrance.

After they had danced for about an hour the colonel suggested that she ask the owner if she could leave early, so she left him at the table and strolled around the bar as if she was going to the owner's office. She lingered in an area where the colonel couldn't see her, counting out a passage of time, and then she returned to the table, saying: "He says it's okay."

"So let's get out of here," he said, taking possession of her with an arm around her waist.

She paused to retrieve her pocketbook from the table, and she let him guide her out of the club. He looked down the street evidently to determine where his driver was waiting with the car, and he whistled at the driver loud enough to wake him up in case he was sleeping. Within a few minutes a car pulled out of a parking spot and headed toward them.

After it had stopped in front of them the driver got out and came around and opened a back door for them. She went in first, feeling something like a soft rug on the floor of the car, and she slid over to the far side of the seat.

When the driver had closed the door after the colonel got in, she followed the script of her role and told the colonel: "I know a hotel where we can go."

"I always go where the girls say," the colonel said. "You know the ropes."

She gave the driver the name and address of the hotel, which luckily wasn't far away because as soon as the car moved forward the colonel tried to kiss her.

Gently, she held him off, saying: "There's no rush. If you wait until we're in the hotel, you can have everything you want."

He leaned away from her but only after swiping a hand across her breasts.

When they got out of the car in front of the hotel the colonel ordered the driver to wait. She guessed that the driver knew from experience how long he would take, so there was no discussion about it.

A man with shaggy hair and glasses was at the desk. The colonel paid him in advance and got a key to a room. It was on the second floor, so there wasn't much time in the elevator for the colonel to grope her, and when they entered the room she was fully intact.

While he was occupied in placing his army hat and jacket on the standing coat rack she made sure that the door to the room was unlocked, and then she said: "I have to use the bathroom."

"I understand," he said, probably believing that she was going to undress and use the bidé.

She took her time in the bathroom, generating sounds of water and waiting for something to happen in the bedroom. It wasn't long before she heard a scuffle, and when she opened the bathroom door she saw Gastón and Facundo standing by the bed on which the colonel was lying prone as if he had passed out.

"Are you all right?" Gastón asked her.

"Yeah, I'm fine," she said, though she could imagine what might have happened if for any reason they were delayed.

She watched as they lifted the colonel from the bed, and she held the door of the room open while they dragged him out into the hall. Before leaving the room she got her pocketbook as well as the colonel's hat and jacket. She waited while they slid the colonel into the elevator, and then she got in after them and pushed the button for the *planta baja*. While the elevator slowly descended she closed her eyes and said a prayer.

She got out of the elevator first and briefly explained to the guy at the desk that her escort had passed out from having too much to drink, and the guy only nodded, barely taking his eyes off the magazine that he was reading. She guessed it was a common occurrence for guys to pass out in this hotel because they came here after drinking.

She held the door of the hotel open while Gastón and Facundo dragged the colonel out, and she stood by while they opened the trunk of Gastón's car.

"Be careful," she told them. "Don't hurt him."

"We won't hurt him," Gastón assured her. "We even brought a pillow for his head."

She looked into the open trunk and saw the pillow, which out of proportion to its use in the kidnapping made her feel better about it.

Back at the *quinta*, wearing baseball caps and masks, Gastón and Facundo helped the colonel get out of the trunk while Catalina watched them from a distance. The colonel was still dazed, so they were able to blindfold him and tie his hands behind his back without a struggle. Then they walked him into the house and led him into the storeroom, which had been cleared and furnished with a mattress for him to sleep on.

"I want to make sure he's all right," Catalina told them.

"Go ahead," Gastón said. "He can't hurt you."

She opened the door and found the colonel sitting on the mattress. He was still wearing his uniform shirt and tie, but he no longer looked like an army officer. He looked like a broken middle-aged man.

"Are you all right?" she asked him.

"Martina?" he growled.

"Yeah, it's me." She felt like telling him she was sorry, which she really was, but she didn't because it would have been absurd.

"So this time I'm the one who got fucked."

She didn't comment.

"What're you going to do to me?"

"We're not going to hurt you. We're only going to ask for ransom money."

A CONTRITE HEART

"Ransom money?" he said with derision. "You think they're going to pay ransom money for a *cabrón* like me?"

"You're a colonel in the army."

"That doesn't mean I have any value. You want to know what I think, young lady? I think they'll be glad to have someone take me off their hands."

"Well, as I said, we're not going to hurt you."

"What if they don't pay you for me?"

No one had thought to ask that question, so she didn't have a ready answer. She finally said: "I guess we'll return you."

"Return me? Like something you bought at a store and decided you don't want?"

She didn't comment.

"Tell me, young lady, do kidnappers have a return policy?"

Again, she didn't comment.

"Who the hell are you guys anyway?"

"We're Montoneros," she lied. When they returned the colonel they wanted him to say it was the Montoneros who kidnapped him.

"You don't have a chance against us, *viste*?"

"Maybe we don't, but we can still fight for what we believe in."

"What do you believe in?"

"Justice," she said.

He snorted with disdain. "When I was your age I believed in justice. I believed in all the ideals that they teach us. But after what I've seen of the world, I don't believe in those ideals. I don't believe in anything."

"You don't believe in God?"

"No. Only fools believe in God."

"Okay. But I'm still going to pray for you."

"Why would you pray for me?"

"Because you need forgiveness, we all need forgiveness."

"*You* need forgiveness? What for?"

"For helping to kidnap you," she said. "It's the worst thing I've ever done in my life."

He made a sound of disgust, then asked: "Could I have a drink of water?"

"Sure. I'll get it for you."

When she went out of the storeroom she ran into Lucio, who asked: "What are you doing?"

"I'm going to get him a glass of water."

"I hope you're not going to take care of him."

"I'm only going to make sure he's all right." As he followed her into the kitchen she sensed that he was worried about something, and she guessed what it was. "I didn't let him touch me if that's what you're worried about."

"Do you blame me?"

"No." She had learned in evolutionary biology that males wanted to control access to their females because they didn't want to help raise the child of another male, so she understood his feelings, but she was still annoyed with him.

"Did he try anything?"

"Of course he tried, but I didn't let him." She found a glass and took it to the sink to fill it with water. "Anyway, Gastón and Facundo arrived in time."

"Thank God," he said. "Don't ever do anything like that again."

"I won't," she promised. "Believe me."

After taking the glass of water to the colonel she left him, and then she joined Lucio in their bedroom. She had a feeling that her words hadn't been enough to assure him, so she made love with him, and lying beside him afterward she sensed that it had assured him. It had also helped to lighten her guilt for using her body to lure a man into captivity.

Since they planned to have the colonel with them for at least a week, Gastón assigned them the tasks of feeding him, exercising him, and keeping him healthy. The task he assigned to Catalina was checking his vital signs, which she did every morning before she went to the *villa* to pursue her mission.

Meanwhile, Gastón worked out a plan for collecting the money, which he revealed to them several days after the kidnapping. As usual, he presented his plan to them at the round table, asking them to hold their questions until he had finished.

"We'll give them specific instructions," he told them. "We'll warn them that if they don't follow these instructions *estrictamnente*, we'll do to the colonel what he did to us in Chaco Province. We'll tell them to be on the north side of a lawn in Palermo Park and not to be anywhere else. I'll park my car on the south side of the lawn, in the driveway of a building where the park stores maintenance equipment. The building is hidden from the lawn by a grove of trees, and I'll stand among the trees where I can watch the lawn without being seen. Facundo will walk onto the lawn from the west side, and he'll go to an ombu tree where they'll deliver the money. He'll have his backpack so he won't take the money away in a bag they give him, which might have a tracker. We'll tell them to have only one guy deliver the money, and in exchange Facundo will give him a note that tells them where they can find the colonel. We'll tell them not to follow Facundo, and I'll be watching to make sure that they don't follow him. Facundo will go to the south side of the lawn, where there's a taxi stand, and he'll get into a taxi. As soon as he's gone I'll go to my car and open the trunk and take out the colonel. I'll leave him in the driveway, and then I'll get out of there. Facundo will have the taxi take him to Plaza Miserere, where he'll get out and go into the subway. To make sure he hasn't been followed, he'll get into a subway car and then get out at the last moment before the door closes, watching to see if anyone else gets out at the same time. If the coast is clear he'll come up to the plaza, where I'll be waiting in my car. Are there any questions?"

"I have a question," Sergio said. "How do we know they'll follow our instructions?"

"We don't know," Gastón said, "but remember, we've warned them that if they don't follow our instructions, we'll do to the colonel what he did to us in Chaco Province."

"So they'll think we're the Montoneros?"

"Right. And they know what the Montoneros have done to kidnapped army officers."

Catalina knew he was referring to the execution of General Aramburu.

"What if they surround the lawn?" Ignacio asked.

"Our instructions tell them to be on the north side of the lawn and not be anywhere else. So if they surrounded the lawn, they wouldn't be following the instructions."

"How exactly will Facundo get the money from them?"

"The guy who delivers the money will take it out of whatever he brought it in, so Facundo can check it, and then Facundo will put the money into his backpack."

"I assume the money will be in dollars."

"It won't be in pesos," Gastón said. "We may be crazy but we're not that crazy."

"So what denomination will the dollars be?"

"One hundred. It's the highest bill there is, and we wouldn't want a higher bill because it wouldn't be easy to use."

The math teacher said: "If we're asking for three hundred thousand dollars in hundred dollar bills, we're talking about three thousand bills."

"It sounds like a lot," Gastón said, "but three thousand bills only weigh about three kilos, and they easily fit into a normal backpack."

After a silence Catalina asked: "What if they don't pay us?"

"What do you mean?"

"What if they don't ransom him?"

Gastón frowned. "Why wouldn't they?"

"Well, maybe they don't want the colonel back," she said, remembering what he had told her.

"Can you tell us why they wouldn't want him back?"

"No, but they could have a reason."

"After what he did to the Montoneros," Lucio said, "he doesn't make the army look good."

"They don't care how the army looks. They have the power."

"Still, it's a possibility," she said. "So what will we do if they don't pay us?"

"I don't know," Gastón said as if he hadn't thought of that possibility. "I guess we'll return him. I don't know what else we could do."

"Will you promise that if they don't pay us, we'll return him unharmed?"

"Yeah, I promise. But they'll pay us. Don't worry."

The next step was for Gastón to write the instructions, which he did with the help of Sergio whose program at the university had included courses on expository writing. They wrote the instructions in block capitals with a standard ballpoint pen on lined pages from the kind of notebook used by students. Gastón read the letter to the group to get their feedback, and after making a few corrections he put the pages into a manila envelope which he dropped into a bin at the main post office in the city. One of the teachers made a dark joke about the unreliability of the postal service, but there wasn't any other way that couldn't be traced.

The instructions set a date for payment of the ransom money that allowed enough time for mail delivery. They made it on a Sunday because there wouldn't be workers at the maintenance building, and if it was a nice day there would be a lot of people in the park, which would limit the scope for military action. According to the weather report it was supposed to be a nice day, but they couldn't rely on the weather bureau any more than they could rely on the postal service, so they had to live with that uncertainty among other things.

When the day of exchange finally came it was indeed a nice day, with a blue sky and only intermittent white clouds. Catalina made sure that the colonel was all right before he was put into the trunk of Gastón's car, blindfolded and with his hands tied behind his back. She noticed that the pillow, which was in the trunk on the night of the kidnapping, was still there, and she gave Gastón credit for this act of consideration.

She was standing by the car when Gastón approached carrying a pistol.

"What's that for?" she asked him.

"It's for self-defense," he told her. "If something goes wrong, I don't want to be captured and tortured."

"I'll pray that nothing goes wrong," she said, watching him get into the car.

Since the time of exchange was set for two in the afternoon she expected Gastón and Facundo to be gone for most of the day, so instead of waiting around for them she and Lucio went to the *villa*, where helping people took their minds off what was happening in the city.

Around five in the afternoon they returned to the *quinta* hoping to find Gastón and Facundo there with the money, but they hadn't yet returned, which made her worry. When Gastón finally returned that evening without Facundo, she knew that something had gone wrong, and she sat with the others at the round table while Gastón told them what had happened, speaking without his usual authority or his usual clarity of exposition.

Their trip to the city was uneventful. When they arrived there they drove to Palermo Park, and Gastón let Facundo off at the west side of the lawn on which the money was to be delivered. He then drove around to the south side and backed the car into the driveway of the maintenance building. With no one around, he opened the trunk to see if the colonel was all right, and then after telling the colonel he would be released soon, he closed the trunk and walked to the grove of trees, where he could observe what happened on the lawn. It was quarter of two, so he had to wait until Facundo was due to appear, and while he waited he scanned the perimeter of the lawn for guys who might have been stationed by the military, but he didn't see any. All he saw was a young woman sitting on the grass with a little boy and a couple on a bench necking.

Right on time he saw Facundo appear on his left, wearing a mask and walking jauntily toward the ombu tree. He stopped in its shade and set down his backpack and stood there, waiting. Within a few minutes a guy in a white tee shirt and jeans, with a flight bag on his shoulder, came into view from the north side of the lawn. With his binoculars Gastón could see that the guy was in his forties with the build of someone who worked out. He watched the guy stop in front of the ombu and swing the flight bag off his shoulder and hand it to Facundo, who unzipped it and took out its contents. After making a quick count of the money, Facundo put it into his backpack and handed a piece of paper to the guy, who turned and headed back to the north side of the lawn.

Facundo emerged from the shade of the ombu tree and was walking toward the south side of the lawn, carrying his backpack. Gastón was watching him, not looking at the guy who delivered the money, so he didn't see him fire the shot. But he saw Facundo jerk as the bullet ripped through him. The guy fired two more shots at Facundo, who by now had crumpled to the ground. Gastón's instinct was to rush out and help his friend, but the guy quickly advanced to Facundo and executed him with a shot to the head. Facundo had fallen onto his backpack, so to get it the guy rolled the body over with the heel of a boot, and then he picked up the backpack and strode in the direction where Facundo had been heading.

Since there was nothing he could do for Facundo, and since there was a strong possibility that the guy might come around to the driveway of the maintenance building, Gastón left the grove and went to his car, which he drove away as quietly as possible. Then, out of danger, he was struck by the enormity of what they had done.

"They killed my friend," he said. "They murdered him in cold blood."

"I don't understand," Sergio said. "By killing him they put the life of the colonel in jeopardy."

"Maybe they think we already killed him," Ignacio said.

"Or maybe," Catalina said, "they don't care if we kill him."

"Well, I think it's clear," Violeta said, "that they're not going to pay us money for him."

"I think you're right," Ignacio said. "So what are we going to do with him?"

"We're going to return him," Catalina said, looking straight at Gastón.

"We can't," he said bluntly.

"Why can't we?"

"Because I killed him."

"Oh, my God," she cried, feeling a stab of pain in her heart. "Please say you didn't."

"I'm sorry, but I did."

Outraged, she said: "*You promised not to hurt him.* And if I hadn't trusted you, I never would have done what I did."

"Why did you kill him?" Lucio asked.

"Because he killed my friend," Gastón said. "Because he wasn't of any value to us. Because he was a liability. All of the above."

"But how was he a liability?"

"We couldn't hold him here indefinitely, and if we returned him they could have gotten some information from him that would lead them to us."

"Like what?" Lucio asked.

"Like how we lured him to that hotel."

"I agreed to take that risk," Catalina said, "so you didn't have to kill him to protect me."

"It wasn't just to protect *you*," Gastón told her, "it was to protect all of us."

"How would killing him protect us?" Ignacio asked. "When they find his body they'll come after us with a vengeance."

"They'll never find his body."

"What did you do with it?"

Looking as if he had regained his composure, Gastón said: "I drove to the marshes beyond Tigre, and I dumped it in the reeds. They'll never find the body there."

"But even if they don't find it," Ignacio said, "he's still missing, and they'll look for him."

"They won't look for him very hard. They obviously don't care about him."

"Maybe they don't, but they'll still look for him."

"Well, they won't find us. They don't know we're here."

"They could track us here. Since you and Facundo were friends, they could make a connection between you. And they'll guess that you were involved in the kidnapping."

"Maybe they will," Gastón said. "But that won't lead them here because no one knows I'm here, not even my family."

"The real estate agent knows you're here."

"But they can't make a connection between us. We don't have a contract or anything."

After a tense silence Violeta said: "My family knows I'm here."

"So? Is there a connection between you and Facundo?"

"I guess there isn't. I only knew him because we were here."

"Then how would they get to your family?"

"I guess they wouldn't."

"Could they make a connection between you and Violeta?" Ignacio asked Gastón.

"They could, but it's not likely," Gastón said. "I recruited her from the students who were followers of Father Francisco. That's how I recruited all of you."

"Well, they could make connections between all of us and Father Francisco."

"Yeah, but you know how many followers he had?"

"I don't know. Hundreds?"

"Thousands," Gastón said. "Including the Montoneros, who they believe did the kidnapping. So they won't come after us, they'll go after the Montoneros."

"Then you believe we're safe here?"

"Yeah. As safe as anywhere."

The meeting ended without any further questions.

Catalina and Lucio waited for the others to leave so they could talk with Gastón. Like the others she worried about their safety, but her main concern was about the role she had played in the kidnapping. She had relied on Gastón's promise not to hurt the colonel, and he had betrayed her, making her feel responsible for the colonel's death. Since this feeling was unbearable she needed to transfer at least some of its weight to him, so as soon as the others were gone she laid into him, yelling: "*Boludo de mierda!* You broke your promise."

"I'm sorry, but I had no choice," Gastón said lamely.

"You had a choice. You could have returned him."

"I explained how returning him would have been riskier than getting rid of him."

"If you'd returned him," she argued, "we would have been in a better situation. But that's not the point. The point is you took a person's life."

"Well, so did they."

"You mean you killed him to get revenge?"

Gastón sighed. "Yeah, I admit that revenge was part of it, but not all of it. I also did it to protect you."

"I heard you say that, but I still don't believe it. I think you're only justifying what you did."

"*Mirá*," Lucio said, "because of the role you got her to play in the kidnapping, she feels responsible for that man's death. Do you understand?"

"I understand," Gastón said. "And I don't feel good about killing him. But I don't feel that bad about it. The colonel was an evil man."

"It's not for us to judge him," Catalina said. "God will judge him. And God will judge us for what we did to him."

"Yeah, I know. Well, it's done, and we have to live with it."

Lucio put an arm around her shoulder and guided her away and into their bedroom, where they talked about it long into the night. He gave her a lot of reasons why she shouldn't feel responsible, beginning with the fact that she had relied on Gastón's promise not to hurt the colonel and ending with the fact that the colonel was an evil man. It helped a little, but not much.

After Lucio had gone to sleep she lay awake for a long time examining her motives for playing a role in the kidnapping and running into a possibility that made her feel even worse. Recalling what she had said to Gastón about his motives, she wondered if it was possible that she had wanted to get revenge for what the military had done to her father.

EIGHT

THEY SPENT MOST of the next day destroying evidence that the colonel had been held at the *quinta*. Two of the guys washed out the trunk of Gastón's car while two other guys took the mattress out of the storeroom and laid it on the lawn and scrubbed it with detergent and left it out in the sun to dry. Violeta rewashed every plate, utensil, and coffee mug that the colonel might have used, and Sergio disposed of the masks that they had worn to prevent the colonel from seeing their faces. Catalina's task was to destroy the black wig and the black dress, which she did in the barrel where they burned garbage. By the end of the day they felt comfortable that if the police came to investigate, they wouldn't find a trace of the colonel.

That week they resumed their mission of helping people in the *villa*. During the day Catalina immersed herself in providing medical services, but at night while she lay in bed awake she couldn't avoid thinking about what she had done, and no matter what she did to justify it, she couldn't allay her feeling of guilt. She could only pray for forgiveness. So after a week of restless nights she welcomed Gastón's suggestion that they all take a day off on Sunday. She slept late, lying next to Lucio, who the previous day had complained about a stomach ache, so when they awoke she asked him how he was feeling. He said a little better, but he still had cramps and he felt nauseous. They agreed that he must have caught a bug in the *villa*, where diseases were rampant, and after advising him not to eat anything for a while she got up and made him some *manzanilla* tea to settle his stomach.

He stayed in bed for the rest of the morning, and around noon she was sitting at the table with the others, eating a sandwich, when a boy appeared on the other side of the screen door that opened onto the patio. From his face and his clothes she could tell that he was from the *villa*, and she got up and went to him to see what he wanted. He told her she was urgently needed because his younger brother had been injured. She asked him how, and he said his brother had fallen onto a piece of sharp rusty metal and cut his arm, which was bleeding a lot. She told him to wait, she would be right back, and she went to the refrigerator and got a vial of tetanus vaccine. Then she went to her bedroom and got her doctor's bag. She would have told Lucio where she was going, but since he was sleeping peacefully she left without disturbing him.

It took about twenty minutes to walk to the *villa*, where the boy led her to a house that looked as if it was under construction. It had one story so far, made of the usual red brick, with a metal roof. She followed him into the house and saw a boy about six years old sitting in a chair with a blood-soaked tee shirt wrapped around his lower arm.

She greeted the mother and went to the boy. She patted his shoulder to comfort him, and kneeling on the cold dirt floor she carefully unwrapped his arm. It was a deep cut, though luckily it had missed a major artery. She opened her bag and got out a package of sterile pads. She cleaned the wound and thoroughly disinfected it. When she prepared to inject the vaccine the boy cringed at the sight of the needle, but she reassured him and distracted him while she gave him the shot. Then she got out the things she needed to close the wound. At the sight of her sewing needle the boy cringed again, but less than before, and he watched patiently with round dark eyes while she carefully stitched up the wound. And finally she dressed it with gauze and tape, which adhered well to his hairless arm. Before leaving she kissed him gently on the forehead and told his mother to have him lie down and take it easy for the rest of the day.

Including the time it took to walk to the *villa* and back, she was gone for less than two hours, but when she approached the *quinta* and didn't see anyone relaxing at the pool, she had a premonition that something had happened during her absence. She walked faster and crossed the patio and went into the house, where she was stunned by the sight of carnage. Some of their bodies were slung over chairs where they had been sitting, and some of their bodies were sprawled on the floor. The table, where they had been eating, was splashed with blood and littered with flesh. The floor was slippery as Catalina rushed into her bedroom, where she found Lucio, lying on his back and riddled with bullet holes.

"Oh God, oh God, oh God," she cried, going to him. Though no one could have survived what they had done to him, she felt his neck for a pulse in the hope that he was still alive, but there was nothing. She laid her head on his bloody chest and stroked his damaged face, saying: "I'm sorry. I'm sorry."

For a long time she stayed there with him overwhelmed by the knowledge that she would never see him again and by the feeling that she was responsible for his death.

Believing that the military had committed the massacre, and that they might return to make sure there were no survivors, she first determined that no one was alive and then she packed her things and left. Because it was Sunday she had to wait a while for a *colectivo*, but it finally arrived, and the long ride gave her time to think. She had enough money for a few nights at a cheap hotel, and that would give her time to arrange a flight to New York. But she didn't have money for a plane ticket, so she would have to get it from someone.

By the time she arrived at Plaza Miserere she had decided that the only person she could ask for the money was Mercedes, who if she hadn't changed her schedule would be in Bajo Flores on Tuesday. If she was careful, she could take a *colectivo* there and avoid being followed. It occurred to her that they would be looking for a girl with black hair, and that might help her elude them long enough to get out of the country.

As she walked around looking for a cheap hotel, she wondered how the military had found them at the *quinta*. Somehow they must have picked up a trail from Facundo, but she couldn't imagine how. And anyway it didn't matter. What mattered was that they were all dead, and keenly feeling the loss of Lucio she wished that she had been there with him.

She finally found a hotel within a short walk from Plaza Miserere.

It had a vacancy, so she checked in, of course using her real name so if they were looking for Martina Aguirre they wouldn't find her there.

The room was small, but it had what she needed—a bed and a bathroom. She put her backpack on the only chair and she hid her doctor's bag under the bed. She couldn't think of any reason why the military would be looking for a doctor, but she didn't want to take any chances.

It was almost seven in the evening, but since it was summer it was still light, so she waited for it to get dark before she went out to get something to eat. She wasn't hungry, but she had to eat something, so she went into a café where she got an *empanada de carne*, which she didn't finish, and a glass of red wine, which she did finish.

As she left the café she decided to call the police and let them know what had happened at the *quinta* because she wanted the bodies of her friends to be collected and given a decent burial. It took her a while to find a pay phone, and she dialed the number that you were supposed to use for emergencies. She told the operator that there had been a shooting in which several people had been killed, she gave them directions to the *quinta*, and she quickly hung up before they could ask her any questions.

Then she went back to her hotel room, and before she went to bed she took a long shower. It made her feel better, though it didn't wash away her sin.

The next morning she left the hotel and went to the same café, where she got a coffee and a roll for breakfast. In the elevator, on her way back to her room, she began to feel nauseous, and she barely made it to the bathroom so she could throw up into the toilet. Since she didn't think you could get food poisoning from coffee and a roll, she guessed it was a stomach bug that she must have caught from Lucio, and she lay down on the bed for a while.

She didn't get up until late in the morning. She didn't feel great, but she felt better, so she went out and walked around, looking for a church. She finally found one, Nuestra Señora de Balvanera, and she went in, noting that the daily Mass was already ended. A few scattered people were in the church, kneeling and praying. She went to a pew in the rear, and she settled into it, at first sitting and then kneeling. With her eyes closed and her hands clasped, she prayed: "*Señor, ten piedad. Cristo, ten piedad. Señor, ten piedad.*"

As she prayed she envisioned herself praying for mercy every day for the rest of her life, and remembering a psalm that prayed for mercy, she sat back in the pew and reached for the missal. It took her a while leafing through the pages to find Psalm 51, which provided words for a penitential prayer. This psalm was known as the Miserere, and she resolved to make it her regular daily prayer. Again she knelt, and she read from the missal: "Have mercy on me, O God, according to your merciful love. According to your abundant mercy, blot out my transgressions. Wash me thoroughly from my iniquity, and cleanse me from my sin. For I know my iniquity, and my sin is ever before me."

After a half hour or so she left the church and wandered around the neighborhood, retracing in her mind the events that had led to the massacre, beginning with Gastón informing them that the money they expected to get from the nonprofit organization was blocked by the military. She had opposed his plan to kidnap the colonel, and she had tried to convince him not to do it, but she ended up playing a role in it, and looking back, she didn't know why. She only knew that she had lured a man to his death, which led to the deaths of all the others, including Lucio. So even if God forgave her, she couldn't ever forgive herself.

It was a long day, and she was glad when it was finally over. She slept a little better than she had the night before, and the next day at least there was something she could do. She could go to Bajo Flores and find Mercedes, whom she was counting on to help her get out of the country. She found the stop for a *colectivo* that would take her there, and when it arrived, filled with people, she boarded it and stood for almost the whole trip, hanging onto the rail and swaying as the bus weaved through traffic on streets that gradually deteriorated.

When she entered the *villa* she felt as if she was coming home after being away for a long time, though it had been only a few months since she left to join Gastón. She was recognized and greeted by people she passed on her way to the house that they used as a base of operations, and she returned their greetings, wishing she had never left but knowing that at the time her only choices were to go with her mother to Rio Cuarto or go with Lucio to the *quinta*, and she could more easily justify that decision than her subsequent decisions.

She found Mercedes at their base of operations, preparing to make a round of house calls. Overcome with emotion at the sight of her mentor, she burst into tears, and Mercedes immediately dropped her bag and came to her and enfolded her in a comforting *abrazo*. After a while Mercedes guided her into a back room that they used as an office, where they both sat down.

"*Qué te pasó?*" Mercedes asked her.

That induced her to open up and tell Mercedes everything that had happened from the time when she had gone to the *quinta* to the time when she had found the bodies of her friends. And Mercedes listened without interrupting her.

"So I have to get out of the country," she said.

Mercedes nodded. "I agree. If you stay, they'll find you sooner or later."

"The thing is, I don't have money for a plane ticket."

"Don't worry. I'll give you the money. And you can pay me back," Mercedes told her with an encouraging smile, "after you become a doctor in New York."

"*Gracias*," she said, bowing her head with gratitude. At that moment she felt a sudden wave of nausea, and she got up and rushed to the bathroom, where she vomited everything inside of her except for her guilt.

"Are you okay?" Mercedes asked her when she returned.

"Yeah. It's only a bug I got from Lucio."

Mercedes put a hand on her forehead, saying: "You don't have a fever. When did this start?"

"Yesterday morning, right after breakfast."

After a moment of reflection Mercedes asked: "Do you use the pill?"

"No, I don't. I mean, I just—" She didn't know what to say.

"Do you mind if I test you?"

"No, I don't mind. But I don't think I'm pregnant."

"You never know." Mercedes got up and found a test, which she administered.

While they were waiting for the results Catalina didn't know what to pray for. If she was pregnant, then she would have a baby from Lucio to love and care for. If she wasn't, then she wouldn't have another life to fear for.

When the test came out positive, Mercedes said: "Well, now you have another reason to leave the country. If they catch you they'll keep you alive until you have the baby, and then they'll kill you and give the baby to an army officer who can't have his own children."

"I understand." Absurdly, this possibility made her wonder if the colonel had children.

"Is there any way they can trace you?"

"Well, for one thing, they can trace me to Father Francisco."

"They can trace all of us to Father Francisco," Mercedes said, "so I wouldn't worry about that. Is there any way they can trace you to the *quinta*?"

"They could find out from people in the *villa* that a doctor was treating them."

"But you're not a doctor, or at least not yet. You're a medical student."

"You mean they'd be looking for a doctor?"

"Yeah. A doctor like me."

She had a spasm of fear. "Oh, God. I hope they won't think that you had anything to do with it."

"Don't worry. They know where I am. It's a long way from here to that *villa*, so it would never occur to them."

"But I don't want to endanger you."

"You won't. You'll be out of the country as soon as possible. Do you have a passport?"

"Yeah," she said. "My father wanted me to have one so in case anything happened to him I could go to New York."

"Your father was prescient," Mercedes said. "Do you know anyone in New York?"

"I have family there. It's my father's cousin. His father and my father's father immigrated from Italy at the same time," she said, retelling the family story. "One of them went to America, and the other came to Argentina. They made a bet on who would do better."

"They did? Well, based on the present situation in Argentina, it looks like the one who went to America won that bet."

"Yeah, I guess." But her heart was still in Argentina, buried with Lucio wherever they put his disfigured remains.

To reduce the risk of the military finding her, Mercedes told her she should come to Almagro and stay there until she departed for New York. In the meantime she should check out of the hotel and dispose of her doctor's bag, which might get attention if she carried it or provide a trail if she left it behind. Before she headed back to the hotel Mercedes gave her the address of her house and told her which *colectivo* to take from Plaza Miserere.

Back at the hotel she got her doctor's bag out from under the bed and wondered how to get rid of it. She finally decided to empty her backpack and put the bag inside it, so she could take it to a place where she could dump it without people knowing what it was. Before putting it into her backpack she examined the contents of the bag to make sure there wasn't anything that could be traced to her, and then she left the room with her backpack.

On her way out of the hotel the man at the desk stopped her and asked if she was leaving, though he shouldn't have worried about not being paid because she had given him enough money in advance for three nights. She told him she was coming back, she only had an errand to do, and that apparently satisfied him. But she was glad that she wouldn't have to spend another night at the hotel.

After walking around she found a dumpster at a construction site, and making sure that no one was watching, she stopped and quickly opened her backpack and dropped her doctor's bag into the dumpster and walked away. If the bag was found by anyone rummaging through the dumpster, there was no way it could be traced to her.

She returned to her hotel room, where she put her clothes and toiletries into the backpack, realizing that they were the only possessions she would have if she arrived in New York. And though it was summer here in Argentina, it was winter there, so she would need to buy a coat and warmer clothes. But she decided to wait until she got there because she believed that no matter how cold it was there, she could get from the airport to her uncle's apartment in the clothes she had, so that wasn't her greatest worry. Her greatest worry was that they would trace her and stop her from getting out of the country.

This time on her way out of the hotel she told the man at the desk that she was leaving, and she waved goodbye to him. She walked to the stop for the *colectivo* that would take her near the street in Almagro where Mercedes lived, and after waiting about ten minutes she was relieved to see it approaching. Half expecting a heavy hand to clamp her shoulder, she boarded the bus and sat down and gave thanks for getting this far.

Mercedes lived in a modest two-story house in a neighborhood that reminded Catalina of the neighborhood where she had grown up. As she rang the bell she realized that as close as she felt to Mercedes, she knew almost nothing about her personal life. She only knew that Mercedes had two adult children whom she had raised without a husband.

The door opened, and Mercedes greeted her warmly, leading her into a cozy living room where music was playing on a stereo. She immediately recognized *La Misa Criolla*, performed by Los Fronterizos, because her mother had played it often. And hearing the familiar music, she felt at home.

Mercedes invited her to sit down in a comfortable chair and offered her a drink of seltzer with lime, which she fixed in the kitchen and brought back into the living room, saying: "What did you eat at the *quinta*?"

"Mostly pasta," Catalina said. "We lived on pasta."

"Well, I'm going to cook you a good meal. You have to eat well for your baby."

Mercedes told her to sit there and enjoy the music while she made dinner, so she took a sip of seltzer and sat back and listened. Toward the end of the Mass she sang along silently with the Fronterizos: "*Cordero de Dios, que quitas los pecados del mundo, ten compasión de nosotros. Cordero de Dios, que quitas los pecados del mundo, ten compasión de nosotros. Cordero de Dios, que quitas los pecados del mundo, danos la paz.*"

"Are you all right?" Mercedes asked, arousing her from a kind of trance.

"Oh, yeah," she said, opening her eyes and realizing that her face was wet with tears.

"Come on. The dinner's ready."

She followed Mercedes into the dining room where a table was set for two, and on each plate was a *bife de chorizo* with roasted potatoes and green beans. She sat down at the table, and if she hadn't reminded herself that she was eating for her baby, she would have been embarrassed by her dispatch of the food.

She offered to help clean up, but Mercedes told her to go into the living room and relax. About ten minutes later Mercedes joined her, sitting in a chair across from her.

"Thanks for the dinner," Catalina said. "I really enjoyed it."

"I'm glad you did. From now on you need to have a balanced diet. You can't live on pasta. And you can't drink wine."

"We didn't drink wine. We couldn't afford it."

"That's good. And you have to get plenty of sleep."

Catalina was touched by this motherly concern, and it made her want to share her feelings, so she said: "I feel lost. I committed a sin, a mortal sin."

"You mean what you did as Martina Aguirre?"

"Yeah. I lured the colonel to his death."

"Well, he wasn't innocent."

"No. He was evil. But that doesn't justify what I did."

After a silence Mercedes said: "Before you did it, you knew it was wrong."

"Oh, yeah. I knew. And I argued against it. I told Gastón that it went against our principles."

"So how did Gastón justify it?"

"He said the military had taken our money, so it would be right to take it back. And he promised not to hurt the colonel."

"So you finally went along with him?"

"I did much more than go along with him," she said. "I played a key role in the kidnapping."

"Do you know why?"

"I think I know why. I believed that if I got involved, then I could make sure that Gastón wouldn't hurt the colonel."

"And you relied on his promise not to hurt the colonel."

"Yeah, I did, but that doesn't absolve me."

After another silence Mercedes asked: "So why do you think Gastón killed him?"

"He said it was to protect us," she said, "but I don't believe it. I think he killed the colonel to get revenge for what the military did to his friend Facundo."

"Can you understand how he might have felt?"

"Yeah, I can understand. After what they did to my father, I can understand how someone might want to get revenge."

"Have you ever wanted to get revenge for what the military did to your father?"

"Sometimes I have. But it's not right to get revenge. It's not what Jesus taught us."

"I know. And we try to live up to what he taught us. But we're only human."

"That's what my mother would tell me."

"When did she tell you that?"

"When I couldn't forgive myself for committing a sin."

"How old were you?"

"Twelve or thirteen. I was going through adolescence," she added unnecessarily.

"It sounds like your mother thought you were being too hard on yourself."

"Yeah, that's what my mother would say. She would say it was only a venial sin."

"I'm sure it was."

Appealing to Mercedes, she said: "But what I did to the colonel was a mortal sin. So I feel lost."

Mercedes nodded sympathetically. "Well, I'm not saying that what you did to the colonel wasn't bad, and I'm not saying it was justified because it wasn't as bad as what the colonel did to the Montoneros, or as bad as what the military did to your father, but if God will forgive anyone in this whole situation, he'll forgive you."

"I hope he will. But the colonel wasn't the only one who was killed because of what I did. The others were killed and Lucio was killed because of what I did."

"No, they were killed because of what Gastón did."

"But the military didn't know he killed the colonel. As far as I know, they hadn't found the body."

"They didn't need to find a body to know what happened to the colonel. They live in a world ruled by revenge, so when they killed Facundo they knew what would happen to the colonel."

"Maybe they did." She paused to think. "I had a feeling that they didn't care about the colonel, *viste*? But if they didn't, then why would they want to kill us?"

"They had to send a message to potential kidnappers. If they'd let you get away with it, they would have lost control of things."

She thought she understood. "So they did it to maintain law and order."

"That's what most people in this country want."

"They don't want justice and peace?"

"They don't want justice and peace at the expense of law and order," Mercedes said. "Which explains why we have a military government."

After reflection Catalina said: "Well, I want justice and peace. So no matter what happens, I'm going to pursue my mission."

"Fine. But you'll have to suspend your mission until you have your baby."

"I know I will. And I want to have her where she'll be safe."

Mercedes smiled. "We only tested to see if you're pregnant. We don't know the sex of the baby."

"I know the sex," Catalina said. "She's going to be a girl."

Mercedes bought her a round-trip ticket to New York because if she had a one-way ticket she might get closer scrutiny from emigration, who were on the lookout for suspicious people fleeing the country. Mercedes also gave her a winter coat to take with her because it would be cold in New York. The flight was on the following Friday at nine in the evening. It was non-stop, but it would still take more than twelve hours, so Mercedes made sure she had reading materials, including a novel in English that would help her with the language.

Since she had to be at the airport at least one hour before flight time, and since it took an hour to get to Ezeiza, they left before seven in Mercedes' jeep, and on the way she told Mercedes what she knew about her uncle and aunt in New York. Her Uncle Angelo was a sculptor who did giant works of metal that corporations bought for the plazas in front of their office buildings or for their lobbies. Her Aunt Elda was a painter who made a living designing book covers for a publishing company. They had no children, and they lived in a modest two-bedroom apartment in the East Village.

The trip to the airport was uneventful, but as they passed the *colectivo* stop near the *quinta* she felt a rush of fear and grief, and she crossed herself as she did as a little girl while passing a cemetery, and she prayed: "*Señor, ten piedad.*"

When they got to the airport Mercedes parked the jeep and went into the terminal with her and waited at a distance while she checked her suitcase. She then proceeded to emigration, where a man with angry dark eyes examined her passport. At one point he frowned as if there was something wrong, and she held her breath and tried not to show concern. But he finally stamped her passport and motioned her through. Before she entered the waiting area she turned and looked back at Mercedes, who gave her a blessing with a nod of her head and a wave of her hand.

She got on the plane and settled into her seat at the window, preparing herself for the long flight. When the plane began to leave the gate she gave thanks for having gotten this far without being stopped, and when it took off she finally relaxed.

NINE

SHORTLY AFTER TAKEOFF the flight attendant came around with a cart and offered drinks. Catalina asked for a seltzer, which she sipped slowly until the flight attendant returned with dinner, giving her a choice of beef or chicken. She chose chicken and took the tray and put it on the pull-down table in front of her, glancing at the man on the aisle to see what he ordered. Luckily, there was no one in the middle seat, which kept them far enough apart so that it was easy to avoid conversation. The last thing she needed was for a curious stranger to ask her questions about where she was from, where she was going, and why she was going there.

The chicken, in a white mushroom sauce, was like nothing she ever saw before. Unlike the whole pieces of chicken that she was used to eating, this chicken was a skinless, boneless breast without any flavor, which explained why it was covered with sauce. The mashed potatoes were powdery, and the carrots were watery. Since she wasn't hungry anyway, she pushed the dinner away from her without finishing it. So this was her first American meal, and she hoped it wasn't typical of what she would eat from now on.

When dinnertime was over she had a choice of two movies, and not knowing anything about them, she decided to watch *All the President's Men*. The movie was about two newspaper reporters investigating a burglary, which they traced to the president, Richard Nixon. As a result, the president was forced to resign. She enjoyed the movie, but she found it very hard to believe that in America a president could be forced to resign for such a minor offense when in Argentina a president could kill thousands of people and not face any consequences. It didn't seem possible that two countries in the same world could be so different.

Too tired to read, she moved her seat back and pulled the blanket over her and tried to sleep. For a long time she was kept awake by her thoughts about the murder of Father Francisco, the bombing in the *villa miseria*, the disappearance of her father, the kidnapping of the colonel, and the massacre of her friends and Lucio, but finally calmed by her dreams about the future with a baby to love and care for, she slipped into oblivion.

She was awakened by the flight attendant offering coffee, which she declined as well as the breakfast. She was feeling a little nauseous, and she was afraid she wouldn't make it off the plane without throwing up. But the crisis passed, and she took out the novel that Mercedes had given her. It was *Terms of Endearment* by Larry McMurtry, a story about the relationship between a mother and her daughter, which occupied her for the rest of the flight.

The plane landed and taxied to the gate, where it took forever to open the door. She waited with the others in economy class for the passengers in first class to disembark, and then she followed the line of people out of the plane and up the ramp and into a corridor that ultimately branched into U.S. citizens and non-U.S. citizens. She waited in the line for the latter, and when she got to immigration she handed her passport along with a card she had filled out on the plane to a big guy with red hair.

"You're from Argentina?" he asked her after looking at her passport.

"Yes," she said, suddenly afraid that they wouldn't let her into the country.

"What's the purpose of your visit?"

"To see my uncle and aunt."

"Where do they live?"

"In New York City."

"How long do you intend to stay?"

"For two weeks." She had written that on the card but she assumed he was testing her for consistency.

He checked the screen of his computer, and then after a long pause he stamped her passport, saying: "Welcome to New York."

Her first priority after getting her baggage was to find a bathroom, where could safely throw up and pee. After meeting those needs she lingered in the stall as if it was a sanctuary. And she gave thanks for getting this far.

She found a pay phone in the main lobby and called her uncle. She hadn't been able to tell him she was coming for fear that a phone call from Mercedes' house might be traced, but her father had exchanged letters with her uncle about her seeking refuge with him if necessary, so the announcement of her arrival in New York wouldn't come out of the blue.

A woman who identified herself as Elda answered the phone and welcomed her as if they were expecting her. Elda gave her their address, speaking slowly and clearly, and told her to take a taxi from the airport, which they would pay for.

Since she had noticed that people were wearing winter coats, she opened her suitcase and took out the coat that Mercedes had given her, and she put it on. When she went outside to the area for taxis she was glad she had a winter coat because it was colder than she had expected, at least thirty degrees colder than in Buenos Aires.

She waited in the line for taxis, and after a while it became her turn. She told the driver where she was going, and he put her suitcase into the trunk. She got into the back of the taxi, he got into the front, and off they went. Within a few minutes they were inching along in heavy traffic on a highway that had more lanes than any highway she had seen before.

"Where ya from?" the driver asked her.

"Italy," she said, not wanting to leave the slightest trail.

"Oh, yeah? Where in Italy?"

"Naples," she said because her paternal grandparents had come from there.

"I bet it's warmer there."

"It is. What is the temperature here?"

"It's thirty-five degrees now."

Having studied science, she knew how to convert Fahrenheit to Centigrade but not in her head, so she settled for knowing it wasn't much above freezing.

"My grandfather's family came from Calabria," the driver said. "And my grandmother's family came from Sicily. I'm Italian on both sides."

"So you must like Italian food."

"Oh, yeah. I love it. We got some good Italian restaurants in New York, though they're probably not as good as what you have in Italy."

She let the conversation peter out, and she rode without talking the rest of the way. It was late morning, and the sun was shining, so she was getting a tour of the city. Her first impression was that everything was rundown, not old enough to be picturesque but definitely looking the worse for wear, and she was surprised by what she saw because she had always believed that America was rich and prosperous.

They went over a rickety metal bridge and headed down a pot-holed street that was lined with dingy buildings, mostly red brick with three or four stories and fire escapes. The farther they went, the poorer the neighborhood looked. Of course she knew that her uncle and aunt were artists, so she didn't expect them to be rich, but she hadn't expected them to be poor either. And she hoped she wouldn't be imposing on them.

Finally the driver stopped in front of a four-story brick building which like most of the other buildings had a fire escape. The meter said she owed sixty dollars, which she had because Mercedes had given her two hundred dollars for travel expenses. Based on her limited experience with taxis in Buenos Aires, she tipped the driver fifteen percent, and he seemed satisfied. He took her suitcase out of the trunk and carried it to the entrance of the building.

With her suitcase she entered the building and stopped at the mailbox panel which had buzzers for the apartments. She found Rinaldi and pressed that buzzer. Within a minute the inner door responded with a sound like a death rattle, and she quickly pushed it open. Since the apartment was 4C she guessed it was on the fourth floor, which in Argentina would have been four floors up, so she paced herself as she started climbing up the stairs, lugging a suitcase that felt twice as heavy as it had before. She was glad to hear someone coming down the stairs, a big man who met her on the second floor. He had long iron-gray hair tied back in a pony tail, a ruddy complexion, and playful blue eyes. Without even verifying her identity he enfolded her in a bear hug, saying: "I'm so glad you made it here safely."

She hugged him in return saying: "Me too."

"Come on," he said, taking her suitcase. "You gotta meet Elda. And none of this uncle shit, okay? You call me Angelo."

"Okay." She was feeling better than she had in a long time.

She followed him up the remaining stairs and into a living room, where a woman was sitting in an easy chair. She had dark full-bodied hair and dark eyes elegantly accentuated by liner in a face that radiated generosity. When she rose from the chair she was shorter than Catalina expected, but even though she was a petite woman her hug was as strong in its own way as Angelo's. "Welcome to our home, honey."

"Your father said you might be coming here," Angelo said. "We didn't know when, but we were expecting you."

"We'd love to talk with you," Elda said kindly. "But you must be tired from your trip, so if you want to lie down and rest, then we can wait."

"I got some sleep on the plane," she told them. "So I will be okay for a while."

"Good. Then have a seat. Would you like some coffee?"

"No, thanks. But I would like a glass of water if that is not trouble."

"I'll get it for you."

Elda had started for the kitchen but paused when Angelo asked: "How's your father?"

Catalina took a long deep breath before she said: "I do not know. They took him away last November, and they disappeared him."

"Oh, my God," Elda cried in anguish.

"Jesus," Angelo said, drawing out the word.

"What about your mother?"

"She went to Rio Cuarto with my brother. That is where she came from."

"Why didn't you go there with her?"

"I was in a relationship with someone, and we could not both go to Rio Cuarto. I mean we could have, but we had a mission."

"Your father's mission?" Angelo asked.

She nodded. "Yes. So we stayed in Buenos Aires."

There was a long silence during which they must have guessed that since the person with whom she had a relationship wasn't here with her, something had happened to him. So she told them he had been killed by the military, and she was pregnant. When she revealed the latter fact they both assured her it was more than okay. They had always wanted children but weren't able to have them, so a baby in their home would be a blessing for them.

Before lying down for a *siesta* she asked them if she could call her mother and let her know she had arrived safely, and they said yes, her mother would be worried about her, so she talked with her mother for the first time since they parted at the airport for the flight to Rio Cuarto, and hearing her voice, her mother said: *"Hija mia. Gracias a Dios!"*

They didn't talk long because she didn't want to run up a big phone bill, but they agreed to talk from time to time so her mother would know how things were going.

By then she was exhausted, and Elda led her to a room in which there was a bed, a bureau, a chair, and an easel that held a painting in progress: a still life with a bottle of wine, a loaf of bread, and a plate of cheese.

"Is this where you paint?" Catalina asked.

"When I have time," Elda said. "I'll move the easel later today."

"Oh, you do not have to. It will not bother me."

"Don't worry. I have a place for it. Now, get some sleep."

When she awoke it was getting dark, and she had to turn a light on. She unpacked her suitcase, hung up her dress in the closet and put the rest of her clothes into drawers of the bureau. Opening the bedroom door, she smelled tomato sauce, and she followed the aroma into the kitchen where she found Elda at the stove stirring a pot.

"Did you get some sleep?" Elda asked her.

"Yes," she said. "Thank you."

Looking at her, Elda said: "You don't have a sweater?"

"I thought I brought one, but I did not see it in my suitcase."

"I'll get you a sweater. We have a landlord who doesn't like to spend money on heat."

"Can I help you?"

"Yeah. You can stir the sauce while I get you something to keep you warm."

She took the wooden spoon from Elda and stood by the pot stirring the sauce. It smelled like the sauce her grandmother made. She hadn't smelled a sauce like that since her grandmother died because her mother, being *gallega*, didn't cook that kind of food.

Returning with a sweater, Elda said: "This is Angelo's. My sweaters would be too small for you."

"Thanks," she said. She pulled the sweater over her head. It was roomy, with a pleasant male smell, and for sure it would keep her warm.

"We'll go out tomorrow and buy some clothes for you," Elda told her, back at the pot. "There's a store on University Place that has everything you'll need."

"Okay. Where is Angelo?"

"He went to his studio. It's over in SoHo. He'll take you there and show you around."

"My father said you design book covers. Where do you work?"

"At a publishing company near Washington Square."

"I will have to find a job," she said, not wanting to be a burden on them.

"For the time being," Elda said, "you have one priority, and that's your baby. I'll line you up with my OBGYN."

"OBGYN?"

"Obstetrics and gynecology. She's a wonderful doctor. She came here as a student from Romania more than twenty years ago, and she stayed here for political reasons. So you have something in common with her." Elda paused. "I saw a lot of her when I was trying to get pregnant. She's a regular OBGYN, but she also specializes in problems of infertility."

"I am sorry you could not—" She really didn't know how to say it.

"That's okay," Elda said. "It looks like God had a plan for me to be a *nonna*."

Angelo returned around seven, and they ate dinner at a butcher block table in the living room. It was *penne bolognese* and a green salad dressed with oil and vinegar. There was enough pasta for twice as many people, and Catalina ate almost as much as Angelo, who probably weighed twice as much as she did. Of course she was also feeding her baby.

The next day Elda took her to a store, which in Buenos Aires wouldn't have been open on Sunday, and bought her a sweater, another pair of jeans, a few pairs of socks, and winter boots. Converting the prices from dollars into pesos, Catalina was surprised that these things were less expensive than in Buenos Aires. Though she had enough dollars left to pay for them, Elda wouldn't let her.

Two days later they celebrated Angelo's sixty-fifth birthday with roast chicken in garlic sauce, potatoes, and zucchini. At the table after dinner he opened gifts from Elda and their friends, and then raising a glass of prosecco he told Catalina that the best gift of all was her coming to live with them in New York and bringing to them an expected *nipotina*.

Their top priority was for Catalina to see a doctor and make sure that things were going well with her pregnancy, but first she had to get health insurance, so Elda arranged for an agent to come to the apartment and enroll Catalina in a plan. The agent, an affable man in his thirties, sat with her in the kitchen and asked her questions about her health and wrote her answers into a form. She had been coached by Elda not to mention that she was pregnant, and since she wasn't showing yet the agent didn't ask about it. He took her temperature and her blood pressure, and after writing the results on the form he gave her a brochure that explained her benefits under the plan. There was a five hundred dollar deductible, but after that her expenses were covered as long as she stayed within the network. He gave her two options of paying for the first year, either the whole premium upfront or in monthly payments. Elda made the decision for her and wrote a check for the whole premium. Holding the check, the agent then launched into a sales pitch for whole life insurance, but Elda cut him off and thanked him and sent him on his way.

As soon as she had received a temporary card in the mail, Elda made an appointment for her with the doctor who had treated her for infertility. Elda walked with her to the corner where she could take a bus to the doctor's office, which was in a building near New York University Hospital. The bus was nothing like the *colectivos* in Buenos Aires, modern and spacious, with plenty of room for the passengers, who rode in silence to wherever they were going. She got off the bus where Elda had told her, and she walked to the building, checking its number to make sure she had the right address. She entered the building, stopped in the lobby to check the listing of offices, and took an elevator to the third floor. In the doctor's office she was greeted by a girl who gave her forms to fill out and asked her what insurance she had. She gave her card to the girl, who made a copy of it, and then she sat down and filled out the forms, which asked a lot of the same questions that the insurance agent had asked her. She gave a positive answer to the question he hadn't asked her.

After a while a nurse led her into an examining room and handed her a hospital gown. The nurse left while she undressed and put on the gown, and then the nurse returned and took her vital signs and asked her a series of questions, holding a clipboard and making notes. The nurse then left her again after telling her the doctor would be right with her.

About ten minutes later the door opened and a woman probably in her early fifties with wavy brown hair and kind brown eyes entered the room. In the opening of her white lab coat a gold cross on a gold chain around her neck was clearly visible. She extended her hand, saying: "Hi. I'm Alina Ciobanu."

"Hi." She shook the doctor's hand. "I am Catalina Rinaldi."

"You're Elda's niece, correct?"

"Yes." She could tell from the way the doctor said it that Elda was a special patient.

"She told me you're from Argentina. Are you by any chance a refugee?"

"I am. Did she tell you that?"

"No, I just guessed. I know you have a military dictatorship there, and I know what it's like to live under a dictatorship."

"My aunt told me you came here as a student."

"That was my father's idea to get me out of Romania. He was a journalist, and he was on their list of undesirables."

So they did have something in common.

"From what Elda told me, I gather that your father was on the military's list."

"Yes. And they disappeared him."

"I'm so sorry," Dr. Ciobanu said with genuine sympathy.

"But I am lucky to have family here."

The doctor nodded. "Elda will be a wonderful grandmother, and Angelo will be a wonderful grandfather. The two of them have gone through a lot together."

She let the doctor guide her through the examination. She had never been subjected to this kind of examination because her parents assumed that she wasn't sexually active, and of course she wasn't until recently. As she followed what the doctor was doing, she was impressed by how thoroughly she examined her.

"Okay," the doctor finally said. "You can get dressed. And then you can come into my office."

She got dressed and left the examining room and went down a corridor to an office where she found Dr. Ciobanu sitting behind a desk.

"Please sit down," the doctor said, indicating the chair in front of her desk.

She sat down and waited for the verdict.

"You're in good health, and everything looks good with your baby."

"Thank God," she said, relieved.

"You've been pregnant for about nine weeks, so your due date should be early October, give or take a week."

"October? My grandmother was born in October."

"The weather's usually good then." The doctor paused. "I understand that you were a medical student at the University of Buenos Aires, and that you completed everything except your residency. Is that correct?"

"Yes. I started my residency, but the doctor who was mentoring me had to leave the country. He was on the military's list."

"I hope he got out of the country safely."

"I think he did. He was coming here."

"So if you're almost a doctor yourself, you should know how to take care of yourself."

"I should," she agreed.

"What about the father? Is he in good health?"

"He was, but—" At this point she started to cry. She couldn't help it.

"I'm so sorry." The doctor, who didn't have to be told what had happened to Lucio, took a tissue from a box on her desk and handed it to Catalina.

"What they did to him was horrible," she cried, letting go. "What they did to my father was horrible. What they did to my priest was horrible."

"I know, I know."

"Why does God let it happen?"

"I'm only a doctor, so all I can say is be thankful that you're safe and healthy, and that you can look forward to having a baby."

She dried her eyes with the tissue, saying: "I am sorry. I did not mean to lose control."

"It's all right. It's good to lose control of those feelings every now and then. So don't hold them in. Okay?"

"Okay." She held the tissue not knowing what to do with it.

"You should make an appointment for one month from now, but if you notice anything that doesn't feel normal, you should see me right away."

"Okay. And thank you for understanding."

"I always try to understand, and I know that when *you* become a doctor, you'll remember what it was like going through the things that you've gone through, and that will help you be a good doctor. God bless you."

The next priority was to deal with her immigration status. Angelo knew a lawyer who specialized in immigration and had helped him with an assistant, an undocumented Venezuelan. He made an appointment with the lawyer, whose name was Sheldon Morse, and he went with Catalina to the lawyer's office. It was in the West Twenties, so they took a crosstown bus over Fourteenth Street and walked the rest of the way.

The office was on the fifth floor of a drab building that looked older than any office building in Buenos Aires, and as they rode up in a creaky elevator Angelo made lifting motions with his hands as if to help it overcome the law of gravity.

They were greeted in the office brusquely by a woman who didn't ask them but ordered them to have a seat, informing them that Mr. Morse was with a client. As they waited, sitting in worn chairs, Catalina looked around the dingy room and noticed on the walls a series of paintings, several different versions of a ceramic pitcher and two ceramic cups. Angelo told her that Elda had done the paintings, and that the lawyer had accepted them as payment for the work he had done for the Venezuelan.

The lawyer finally emerged from his office, guiding his client with a hand on his shoulder, speaking in a dialect of Spanish that she could barely understand. When the client had left the office, the lawyer turned to them and said: "*Angelo, amico mio. È bello vederti.*"

"*È bello vedere anche te.* This is Catalina, my niece."

"*È un piacere incontrarti. Parli italiano?*"

She more or less understood what he had said, especially the last two words. "No, I do not. I speak Spanish."

"I thought everyone in Argentina was Italian." He was a tall man with crinkled gray hair and inquisitive eyes that looked as if they were peering over the top of a wall.

"Most of us are. At least I am half Italian," she added. She was surprised that Angelo spoke Italian because except for a few words she hadn't ever heard her father speak it, and he was the same generation as Angelo.

"Come into my office. You speak English, right?"

"A little," she said, following the lawyer.

They sat down at an oblong conference table, with the lawyer at the head. He began by saying: "You can call me Sheldon. Okay?"

"Okay." She wouldn't have called him by his first name in Argentina.

"I understand that you came to this country to escape from a military regime that's killing people by the thousands, and that you want asylum, right?"

"Right."

"So what's the true story?"

"The true story?"

"Yeah, tell me why you had to leave Argentina. I gotta know the true story," he explained, "so I can make up the right story."

Confused, she said: "I had to leave Argentina because I am on a list of people that the military want to get rid of."

"Why are you on this list?"

"Because I was helping the poor."

Sheldon shook his head and glanced at Angelo, saying: "That won't cut it. You don't get put on that kind of list for helping the poor."

"You do in Argentina."

"Let me explain," Sheldon said patiently. "Our system for granting asylum has two basic requirements. You gotta establish that you fear persecution in your home country, and you gotta prove that you would be persecuted there on the grounds of race, religion, nationality, political opinion, or social group. You understand?"

She nodded. "I think so."

"Now, you're white, and Argentina is a white country, so you can't prove that you would be persecuted on the ground of race. Are you Catholic?"

"Yes."

"Argentina is a Catholic country, so that won't help. If you were Jewish, you could claim that you would be persecuted on the ground of religion because I understand that your military government is anti-Semitic."

"It is," she said, thinking of Dr. Rosenberg.

"Are you an Argentine citizen?"

"Yes."

"So you can't claim that you would be persecuted on the ground of nationality. And since social group is hard to define, your only viable ground is political opinion."

She understood.

"Now, where do you stand politically?"

"On the left," she said. "Where my father stood."

"Your father? Is he on their list?"

"He was," she said, trying not to cry. "They disappeared him."

Sheldon frowned. "They disappeared him?"

"They took him away," Angelo said, "and no one has seen him or heard from him since."

"Oh, man. I'm sorry. Why did they do that?"

"My father was a deputy in Congress. He was a socialist, and they want to get rid of everyone who might be a Marxist."

"Well, that won't help. They don't like socialists in this country either. So we need to find another angle. What's your position on human rights?"

"I believe in human rights."

"Good. And you took a position against the military on that issue, didn't you."

"Yes, I did," she said, following his lead.

"So we're going to argue that the military is persecuting you because of your position on human rights. But we need some evidence of your being persecuted on that ground. Can you give me any evidence?"

"They killed my priest because of his position on human rights. They killed my father for that reason. And they killed my friends for that reason."

"Did they kill any particular friend?"

She glanced at Angelo, who nodded for her to go ahead. "They killed the father of the baby I am going to have."

"You're pregnant?" Sheldon said with eyes lighting up. "Well, that could help."

"How could it help?" Angelo asked.

"There aren't many people seeking asylum who are going to have white babies. I mean, I'm assuming the father was white."

"That's disgusting," Angelo said, making a face.

"It's not me, it's our country," Sheldon said. "We're racist to the core."

"So if I was not white, being pregnant would not help me?"

"It probably wouldn't. I'm sorry," Sheldon said, looking at Angelo, "but we have to play every card we have. You know, they turn down two thirds of the applicants for asylum. And if they turn her down, they'll send her back to Argentina."

Feeling a stab of fear at the thought of their sending her back to Argentina, she resolved to do whatever it took to stop that from happening.

"So what's the process?" Angelo asked.

"We present her claim to an asylum officer, who could grant her asylum or refer her application to an immigration judge. Of course it'll be much better if the officer grants her asylum. So we want to make her case as strong as possible."

"How can we do that?"

"By presenting evidence that she has a well-founded fear of being persecuted." Sheldon turned to her. "You say they killed your priest, they killed your father, they killed your friends, and they killed the father of your baby. Do you have any records to prove it?"

She racked her brain. "There were newspaper articles about the priest and about my father. And maybe there were articles about my friends."

"Could you get copies of these articles?"

"I could ask my mother to try to get them."

"Where's your mother?"

"In Argentina."

"Well, I don't want your mother to get into trouble," Sheldon said. "So I'll try to get them. I just need the approximate dates and the newspapers that might have run the articles."

She gave Sheldon this information to the best of her ability.

"Okay," he said. "I'll put the case together, and we can meet again to review it."

"From the time you present her application," Angelo said, "how long will it take for them to make a decision on it?"

"Oh, I don't know. With all the refugees from Vietnam, they have a mountain of applications. But they don't have many cases like this, so my goal is to get a decision before she has her baby. When's your due date?" Sheldon asked her.

"Early October."

"So we'll try to get a decision by then."

"A positive decision," Angelo said

"Of course. I don't work on cases to lose them."

Of all the things that Sheldon had said she was most reassured by this statement, believing he would do whatever it took to win her case.

TEN

ONE MORNING, AFTER she had been in New York for a few weeks, Angelo took her to his studio in SoHo. They walked there because that was how Angelo got to his studio every day unless it was raining hard or snowing. He said he needed the exercise, and walking gave him time to think.

Catalina used every chance she had to familiarize herself with the city, so she paid attention to their route in case she had to go to the studio on her own for any reason. After leaving the apartment building they headed west to First Avenue and then they went south to Houston Street, where again they headed west. As they walked along she also used the chance to talk with Angelo and get to know him better. She began by asking: "Did you grow up in New York?"

"No," he said definitely. "I grew up in Brooklyn."

"Is Brooklyn a different city?"

"It was until Manhattan annexed it. But I still consider it a different city."

"Where in Brooklyn did you live?"

"We lived in Red Hook, which long ago was a busy port, but by the time I came along it was a poor area."

"So you grew up poor?"

"Dirt poor. But we survived. My father did odd construction jobs, and my mother cooked for a rich family."

"Was your mother Italian?"

"No, she was Norwegian, or part Norwegian. She was the daughter of a Norwegian sailor. At one time there were a lot of Norwegian sailors in Red Hook. I get my blue eyes from my mother," he added.

Having studied genetics, she said: "You did not get your blue eyes only from your mother. Your father must have had a gene for blue eyes."

"Yeah, someone pointed that out to me."

They stopped at Second Avenue to wait for the light.

After thinking about it she said: "If your father had a gene for blue eyes, then my grandfather could have had one because they were brothers."

"It could have been those Germans who came from the north and sacked Rome."

"Did they get to Naples?"

"I don't know. They probably did. If they made it all the way to Rome, they could have easily made it to Naples."

They crossed the street.

"Have you ever been to Italy?" she asked.

"I went there with the army in 1943, and I stayed there after the war."

Since they had celebrated his birthday she knew that Angelo was sixty-five, and she figured that he was around thirty in 1943. "Why were you in the army?"

"Because I was drafted. I was at the upper end of the draft age, but they were desperate for cannon fodder."

"Cannon fodder?"

"Men who if they were killed in combat wouldn't be a great loss to anyone."

She got the idea. "Who did you fight against in Italy?"

"Mainly the Germans. The Italians were sick of war by then, and most of them welcomed us. They hated the Germans."

"How long were you there?"

"Almost seven years. Long enough to really learn the language. When I look back," he reflected, "being drafted was the best thing that happened to me. It got me out of Red Hook, and it got me into the world of art."

"Where did you live?"

"In Florence, surrounded by the works of Donatello and Michelangelo."

She had never studied art, but she recognized the names. "Is that when you decided to be a sculptor?"

"Yeah. When I finally came home I went to the Pratt Institute on the GI bill, and I studied sculpture there. I even got a degree," he added as if he couldn't believe it.

They were heading south on Lafayette Street when her mind returned to the subject of blue eyes, and she said: "You know, if my grandfather had a gene for blue eyes, then my baby could have blue eyes."

"How do you figure?"

"The father had blue eyes."

"So it's possible. Do you care what color eyes your baby has?"

"No, not really. But it would be nice if she had blue eyes like her father."

"Did Dr. Ciobanu tell you it's a girl?"

"No. But I know it is."

Angelo laughed. "That's what I really love about women. You know things that men don't have a clue about."

When they turned into the street where his studio was she noticed that the buildings were old and elegant, most of them with five stories and some of them with columns and vaulted windows. They stopped walking while Angelo gave her the history of the area. From soon after the Civil War to soon after World War II it was an important center of manufacturing and distribution, mainly in the textile industry. When that industry moved south for cheaper labor the area went into decline. In the 1960s the city planned to run an expressway through it, but the plan was stopped by preservationists, and the large spaces in abandoned buildings attracted artists, some of whom lived in their lofts in violation of the industrial zoning. The city tried to prevent them from living there, but the artists organized and won that battle. SoHo became the center of art in New York City, but its success was attracting real estate developers who cared only about money, so now it was being gentrified, and it was already too expensive for artists who weren't already established.

Angelo unlocked the large front door of his building, and he led her across a hallway into a freight elevator, which carried them up to the second floor. Getting out of the elevator, she was awed by the space and the height of the ceiling. She quickly realized that he needed this space because in the middle of the floor, about ten feet high, was a work in progress, a balancing act of metal blocks. Angelo explained that the work had been commissioned by a bank for placement in the middle of its plaza.

"So you sell your work to banks?" she said, a little surprised.

"Yeah, banks are my best customers. You know," he said, "the great artists of the Renaissance sold their work to banks."

"They did?"

"The Medici were in banking, among other activities that made them rich. It doesn't take long to figure out that art goes where the money is, which is why it moved from Italy to Spain, to the Netherlands, to Britain, and finally to America."

"But you do not do it for money."

"No. I do it for people to see and enjoy. And if my work is in the plaza of a major bank, a lot of people will see it."

She walked around the work in progress, seeing it from all sides. "Those blocks must be heavy. How do you lift them?"

"With my muscles," he joked, flexing them. "If you look up, you'll see what I use for lifting heavy pieces."

"Oh, yes." She saw a crane hanging from a beam from which it could be rolled into position.

"Until now I've specialized in making big works, but I have some ideas for smaller works, which people could put in their offices. I have a prototype over here."

She followed him to a corner, where a bundle of reeds made of copper stood on the floor.

"Go ahead and touch it."

She touched it, and the reeds rippled as if they had been stirred by a breeze.

"It's called kinetic sculpture," he told her. "Because it moves."

"I like it," she said, not knowing why. She touched the reeds again, and they moved.

"This type of work will open up a new market for me, and as I get older, it's harder to lift the heavy pieces, even with the help of a crane."

She walked around, looking at photographs on the walls that

showed his works in front of office buildings in different locations, including New York, Boston, Chicago, London, Frankfurt, Tokyo, and Sydney. From the way that her uncle and aunt lived, she knew they weren't rich, but seeing these signs of commercial success she felt better about their supporting her.

On the way home he took her on a tour through Little Italy, where on Sullivan Street she saw the church of St. Anthony of Padua. He told her that the feast of St. Anthony was celebrated on this street, which was lined with food vendors and thronged with people eating pizza and cannoli and zeppole.

Seeing the church made her ask: "Is there a church near your apartment?"

"Oh, yeah. There's a big church not far from us."

"You do not go to Mass there?"

"No, we don't. My father was an atheist, and my mother was a Lutheran, but she didn't have time to go to church. She worked on Sundays."

"My grandfather was also an atheist."

"They were brothers, so they had the same experiences growing up. My father hated the church in Italy because he said it exploited poor people."

"My grandfather said the same thing. But my father was—how do you say? He did not know whether or not he believed in God."

"So he was agnostic."

She repeated the word to learn it. "But then he met my mother, who converted him, so I was raised as a Catholic."

"When I met Elda she converted me. But then she lapsed."

"Lapsed?"

"She stopped going to Mass. When we were trying to have a baby, she went every day. She prayed and prayed for God to give her a baby. And when it didn't happen she lapsed."

"Well, maybe I can get her to go with me."

"If you could, it would be good for her. And your being here is good for her. She's so happy about the baby you're going to have."

"*Si Dios quiere,*" she said reflexively.
"What does that mean?"
"If God is willing."
"Oh, yeah. *Se Dio vuole.* But you're in the hands of a competent doctor, so everything's going to be fine."
"I hope so."

He put his strong arm around her shoulder and guided her onto Houston Street, making her feel that she was in the hands of a loving family.

That evening, as they were in the kitchen cleaning up after dinner, she asked Elda to go to church with her. Elda demurred and pointed out that she couldn't take communion because she hadn't gone to confession in years. Catalina told her that since she herself hadn't gone to confession in a long time, they were in the same position. And she finally got Elda to agree to go to church with her the next Sunday.

It was a big church, as Angelo had said, and it was more than half filled for the eleven o'clock Mass. They went to the right side aisle, and Elda chose a pew near the back where they wouldn't be in the priest's line of vision. Catalina pulled out the kneeler and knelt down, beginning her silent prayer with the Miserere: "Have mercy on me, O God, according to your merciful love. According to your abundant mercy, blot out my transgressions. Wash me thoroughly from my iniquity, and cleanse me from my sin. Purge me with hyssop, and I shall be clean. Wash me, and I shall be whiter than snow."

As she rose and settled onto the pew she didn't feel clean, she didn't feel whiter than snow. She felt dirty, she felt blacker than tar, and she almost regretted coming to church, where her sin was ever before her. She looked at the bulletin that an usher had handed her, and she saw that it was the fourth Sunday of Lent, and she realized that in her scramble to escape from Argentina she had missed Ash Wednesday. She hadn't even known it was Lent. So she resolved to make her usual Lenten sacrifice of giving up beef, which in Argentina wasn't easy.

She got the hymnal from the back of the pew in front of her, and she found the hymn for the procession, which consisted of a priest following two altar servers. She didn't know the hymn, but she followed it and began singing along on the last stanza. She followed the introductory rites, joining in the general confession, which she had to read from the missal so she could say it in English. She followed the Collect in the missal but had a little trouble understanding it. The first reading was about the selection and anointing of David to be the king of Israel. The psalm was "The Lord is my shepherd," which she had no trouble understanding. The epistle was from Ephesians, and she recognized the words: "You were once darkness, but now you are light in the Lord. Live as children of light, for light produces every kind of goodness." The gospel was about Jesus restoring sight for a man who had been blind from birth. She had heard this reading many times, and she was heartened as always by what Jesus did after telling his disciples: "I am the light of the world."

She listened closely to the homily, which dealt with the themes of the readings. The priest spoke slowly and clearly as if he was conscious of the fact that for many of his congregation English was a second language, so she had no trouble understanding him. The main themes were the line of David that led to Christ the King, the role of the shepherd in leading people, and the transformation from darkness to light, from sin to forgiveness. She was mindful of the sins that the military had committed as well as the sin that she had committed, and she didn't see how she could forgive the military or herself. But the point of the gospel was that miracles happen, so she prayed for such a miracle.

She and Elda knelt during the Eucharistic prayer, they stood and held hands for the Lord's prayer, and they joined in singing: "Lamb of God, you take away the sins of the world, have mercy on us." They knelt again for another prayer, but they didn't join the people who lined up to take communion, and it felt as if they were somehow bonded by their exclusion from the reason for attending Mass.

As she watched the people returning from communion with downcast eyes and hands folded, she noticed that many of them had brown skin and indigenous features like the people in the *villas*, and at least that made her feel at home. It made her remember the Masses celebrated by Father Francisco, with Lucio as his altar server, looking like an angel.

Outside the church Elda put an arm around her waist and thanked her for taking her back to church. She said she had noted the hours for confession, and she offered to join Catalina in going to confession so that next time they could take communion.

At the next opportunity she and Elda went to confession. She told the priest about her role in the kidnapping, about what had happened to the colonel and her friends, and she went away with a feeling that the priest didn't appreciate the gravity of her sin because he only gave her a routine penance. But at least having made a confession she could take communion, and from then on she and Elda went to Mass every Sunday.

One evening she and Elda were in the living room, which had the dining area at one end, the sitting area in the middle, and the painting area with the easel at the other end. She was sitting on the sofa, and Elda was sitting in the easy chair she always sat in, reserving the other chair for Angelo, who hadn't yet come home from a meeting with his agent. The dinner was ready, one of the hearty soups that Elda made every week, which would be accompanied by a loaf of crusty bread that she had bought on her way home from work at a bakery on Sullivan Street. Elda had a glass of red wine, and Catalina had a mug of herbal tea. They were talking about their resumption of going to Mass when Elda asked: "What you confessed before you could take communion—is that why you had to leave Argentina?"

"Yes, it is." She wasn't surprised that Elda had guessed there was a connection.

"I know you confessed to a priest, but whatever it is, if you tell me about it I promise I won't judge you. And it might help."

Realizing that the time had come, she told Elda everything from the time when the money for their mission was blocked by the military government to the time when she returned from the *villa* and found the bodies of her murdered friends, including the father of her baby.

Elda listened, not saying a word, and then after a long silence she said: "So you feel guilty for what you did in the kidnapping."

"Yes. If I had not done it, all those people would be alive."

"But you did it for a good cause."

"That does not justify it."

"You don't have to justify it," Elda told her. "You only have to repent, and God will forgive you. In fact, since you obviously *have* repented, God has already forgiven you."

"Maybe he has," she said. "But I have not forgiven myself."

"You should. You should give yourself a break."

"A break?" Angelo asked, entering the room. "What are you talking about?"

Catalina hesitated, feeling reluctant to tell him.

"I think you should tell him," Elda said.

"Tell me what?" Angelo asked, settling comfortably into the other easy chair.

"The reason why I had to leave Argentina."

"I thought it was because you were on the military's list."

"It was. But I was on their list for a reason that had nothing to do with my father," she said. And then she repeated what she had told Elda.

When she was finished Angelo said: "You were in a war, and when you're in a war you do things you wouldn't ever do in a normal situation."

"He's speaking from experience," Elda said.

"I did things in the war that no one should have to do. And I'll never forget them. But I forgave myself for what I did. I realized that in those situations I had no choice."

"You mean that God took away your free will?" she asked, considering the possibility.

"He didn't have to take it away. He put me in situations where I had no choice, so it wasn't a question of free will. I did what I had to do."

"Well, maybe that applies to me," she said. "I have to think about it."

She did think about it. But after lying in bed awake for a long time that night she concluded that she hadn't been in a situation where she had no choice. She had a choice, and she could have decided not to play a role in the kidnapping, but she did, though she didn't fully understand why.

Three weeks later she and Angelo met again with Sheldon Morse, who in the meantime had been busy. With pride he showed them copies of articles from newspapers about the murder of Father Francisco, the disappearance of her father, and the massacre of her friends. These articles were from reliable sources, including the *New York Times* and the *Buenos Aires Herald*, a respected English-language newspaper that courageously opposed the military regime, so they provided credible evidence to support her case.

Sheldon had scheduled a meeting with an immigration officer for early June, and he met with Catalina several times during the weeks leading up to that meeting. Anticipating the questions that the officer would ask her, Sheldon wrote a script for her, and he had her rehearse her answers until she knew them as well as an actress knew her lines for a role in a play. He also threw her unexpected questions, which helped to prepare her for anything that the officer might ask her. Sheldon impressed on her the fact that in making her case she had to overcome the bureaucratic predilection for turning it down.

When the day of the meeting finally arrived she was very nervous, but Sheldon went with her to the building where the immigration department had offices, and though he couldn't be with her at the meeting he would be right outside in the waiting room, transmitting support to her.

The officer kept her waiting for more than a half hour, which made her even more nervous. When she was allowed to enter his office she found him sitting at a table with papers spread in front of him, including what looked like copies of newspaper articles. He was a trim man in his mid-fifties, with short gray hair and steely gray eyes.

"You may sit down," he told her, indicating a chair across the table from him.

She sat down and faced him. She noticed a tag clipped to the left pocket of his shirt, which said his name was Alan Klein.

"What is your name?" he asked her.

"Catalina Rinaldi."

"Where were you born?"

"In Buenos Aires, Argentina."

"What's your date of birth?"

"September 20, 1952."

"When did you arrive in New York?"

"On March 11 of this year."

"Where are you staying?"

"With my uncle an aunt, Angelo and Elda Rinaldi."

"Are they supporting you?"

"Yes, until I can support myself."

He must have noticed that she was pregnant because by now she was showing, so she expected him to ask when her baby was due, but so far he hadn't. In fact, he hadn't asked any questions about her health. Instead, after pausing to review a paper, he got to the point and asked her: "Why did you leave Argentina?"

"I left Argentina," she said, following her script, "because I was being persecuted by the military government."

"How were you being persecuted?"

"I was a medical student at the University of Buenos Aires. I completed all my courses, and to get my degree I only had to do one year of residency in a hospital. I started doing a residency, but the military arrested the doctor who was my mentor."

"What was the doctor's name?"

"David Rosenberg."

"What happened to him?"

"They held him overnight, and they questioned him. When they let him go the next morning he decided to leave the country. He had a wife and two small children."

"Why do you think the military arrested him?"

"Because he was a Jew. The military are anti-Semitic," she told the officer. If he was a Jew, that would help.

"What happened to you then?"

"I was told by the hospital that they did not have a position for me, so I could not continue my residency. I tried to get a residency at other hospitals, but they did not have a position for me."

"Were you a good student at medical school?"

"I was in the top five percent of my class."

The officer frowned as if he didn't understand. "Then why didn't those hospitals have a position for you?"

"Because I was on the military's list."

"The military's list?"

"The list of people they wanted to get rid of."

"But if you were a good student at medical school, you had the potential to be a good doctor, so why would the military want to get rid of you?"

"Because I opposed what they were doing to people."

"What were they doing to people?"

"They were arresting them and torturing them and killing them," she said, trying to control the tremor in her voice.

"And how did you oppose the military?"

"By helping people who lived in *villas miseria*."

"*Villas miseria?*" the officer said, looking perplexed.

"That is what we call the slums in Buenos Aires. The people who live there are dirt poor," she said, using an expression she had learned from Angelo.

"So how were helping people in the slums?"

"By providing medical services for them."

"How were you doing that?"

"We had a clinic in one *villa*, and I was working with a doctor there. But the military bombed the clinic, and from then on we could only make house calls."

"Why did the military bomb the clinic?"

"To make it harder for us to provide medical services."

The officer shook his head, saying: "I don't get it. Why would the military want to make it harder for you to provide medical services for people in the slums?"

"Because most of the people who live in the slums are at least partly indigenous, so they are not white," she explained, following Sheldon's advice to play the race card.

"Are you saying the military are racist?"

"Yes. The military want Argentina to be a country only for white Europeans."

The officer paused as if to understand clearly what she had told him. "So you're saying that the military are anti-Semitic and racist. Correct?"

"Correct."

"Okay." He paused. "I have copies of newspaper articles about what the military did to your priest, your father, and your friends. Could you tell me why the military did those things?"

"Because they did not like what my priest, my father, and my friends were doing?"

"What were they doing?"

"My priest was bringing religion to poor people. And though the military profess to be Catholic and have the support from higher levels of the church, they think religion should not be brought to poor people."

"What was your father doing?"

"He was serving as a deputy in Congress, which the military closed down. The military do not believe in democracy, and my father did. He believed in government of the people."

"What were your friends doing?"

"They were helping poor people like I was."

The officer moved directly on to the next question. "So if we sent you back to Argentina, what do you think the military would do to you?"

"They would kill me."

"Why do you think that?"

"Because they killed my priest, they killed my father, and they killed my friends. You have the evidence in front of you."

The officer looked down at the newspaper articles, and he shuffled them around before saying: "I noticed that you're pregnant. Would the military also kill your baby?"

"No. They would wait until I had my baby, and then they would kill me and take my baby."

"What do you think they would do with your baby?"

"They would give it to a military officer who could not have his own children."

"If that happened," the officer asked, looking at her closely, "what kind of life do you think your baby would have?"

"A terrible life," she said with feeling. "My baby would live under a dictatorship, with no rights and no opportunities. She would probably end up being a slave."

The officer didn't comment.

"If I could stay here, my baby could live under a democracy, with rights and opportunities."

"If you could stay here, what would you do for a living?"

"I would complete my medical degree," she said, "and I would be a doctor here like I was going to be there before the military started persecuting me."

The officer wrote down something on a paper in front of him. "I have one final question. Are you a Marxist?"

"No, I am not. I am a Catholic. I believe in God, and Marxists do not believe in God. They only believe in material things."

"I assume your priest was also a Catholic, but what about your father and your friends?"

"They were all Catholics like me. They were not Marxists."

"But if they were Catholics, why did the military want to get rid of them?"

"Because the military are not Catholics. They only claim to be Catholics to get the support of the church."

"If they're not Catholics, then what are they?"

"They are men who want power, and they will do anything to get it. And anything to keep it," she added. "They have already killed thousands of people, and they will keep killing people to stay in power."

"Okay, Ms. Rinaldi," he said after a long silence. "You may go now. Thank you."

When she went out to the waiting room she saw Sheldon there for her, and she went to him, feeling drained.

"How did it go?" he asked her.

"I think it went well," she told him. "At least I played all the cards that you told me to play."

He rose from his chair and took her hand, saying: "Good girl. Come on, I'll buy you lunch. I know a great Chinese restaurant only a few blocks from here."

After her meeting with the immigration officer the time passed slowly as she waited for a decision on her application for asylum. It was bad enough during the week days because Elda was at work and Angelo was at his studio so she was alone in the apartment. She spent some of the time reading but she spent most of the time watching television, which she justified because it was helping her improve her English. But it was worse at night when she almost always had trouble sleeping. Alone in the dark, she prayed that her application for asylum would be approved but even as she prayed she acknowledged the possibility that she deserved to be sent back to Argentina as a punishment for her sin. What usually saved her from despair was her faith that an innocent baby didn't deserve to be taken from its mother and given as a prize to an army officer. But when she became acutely conscious of her sin and its consequences her faith was overwhelmed by fear, and in that state of mind she talked with Father Francisco, who she imagined sitting at her bedside.

"*Bendíceme, padre,*" she would say, "for I have sinned."

"Tell me how you've sinned," he would say.

"I used my body, a temple of the Holy Spirit, to lure a man to a hotel so that we could kidnap him."

"What kind of man was he?"

"An army colonel. An evil man. He tortured and killed twenty of your former students."

"So he was an evil man, but why did you kidnap him?"

"To raise money to build a church, a clinic, and a school in a *villa miseria.*"

"Your end was good, but your means was bad, and the end doesn't justify the means."

"I know it doesn't. And I was against the kidnapping, but I finally went along with it. I not only went along with it, I played a key role in it."

"What made you do that?"

"I don't know," she would say. "I guess I felt that since they kidnapped my father, it was all right to kidnap one of them. I guess I felt it would be justice."

"But it's not your place to mete out justice."

"I know it's not."

"And there's a thin line between justice and revenge."

"I know."

"So what happened to the man you kidnapped?"

"Gastón killed him."

"Gastón? Oh, I'm sorry to hear that. I thought he had great leadership potential."

"Well, he was our leader. And when he went to collect the ransom with his friend, the guy who brought the money killed his friend. So he killed the colonel. He said he did it to protect us, but I think he did it for revenge."

"It sounds like revenge."

"I know I did an evil thing, father, and I feel I deserve to be punished. But I'm going to have a baby, and I don't want her to be punished for something I did. I mean, she's innocent. So please tell me that my baby won't be punished."

"How do you think she'd be punished?" he would ask.

"If they send me back to Argentina," she would say, "the military will kill me. They'll wait until I have my baby, and then they'll kill me. And they'll give my baby to an army officer who can't have children."

"But if they gave your baby to an army officer, it wouldn't necessarily be a punishment for her."

"You mean she could end up with a better mother?"

"It's possible. But knowing you, I don't believe she *would* end up with a better mother. I just want to make sure that if they don't send you back to Argentina, you'll realize what a blessing you've received. And you'll be thankful."

"After what I did, do you believe I deserve such a blessing?"

"I believe you do. And you should know that God has already forgiven you."

"Maybe he has, but I haven't forgiven myself."

"Well, that's up to you. Remember how we pray: 'Forgive us our sins as we forgive those who sin against us.' Forgiving others is the key to it."

She would lie there in bed for a long time, pondering what he had said. She understood it, but she didn't see how it would work for her. She couldn't imagine forgiving the people who had killed her priest, her father, her friends, and the father of her baby.

The summer dragged on, and as she gained weight it got harder for her to climb the stairs to the apartment. It also got harder for her to live with the uncertainty about her application for asylum. At one point in early August she called Sheldon and asked him why it was taking so long, and he told her it was good that they hadn't made a quick decision because if they had, they would have been likely to decline her application. The longer it took the more likely they were to approve it. So not to worry, the process was going as he hoped it would. And not to expect a decision in August because no one worked during that month.

Finally, one evening in early September, Elda came home from work and brought the mail from their box in the vestibule of the building, and she had an envelope that looked official. Holding her breath, Catalina opened the envelope and read the letter, which approved her application and gave her instructions on what to do next.

She hugged Elda, who hugged her back. With tears in her eyes she thanked God, she thanked Sheldon, and she thanked Elda and Angelo. What mattered above everything was that she would be able to keep her baby and to raise a child in a country where they weren't torturing and killing people, where they weren't making people disappear.

Her baby arrived not long after the due date, and it was a girl with blue eyes like her father. Again she thanked God, and she thanked Dr. Ciobanu, who had seen her through a pregnancy that with all her stress could have gone wrong.

"You're a *nonna* now," she told Elda, who along with Angelo had waited in a visitors room at the hospital for the delivery.

"And I'm a *nonno*," Angelo said. "What's her name?"

"Lucía." It was the name she had in mind since learning that she was pregnant because she wanted a name for the baby that recalled the father's name. And she hoped that Lucio, wherever he was, could see his daughter.

ELEVEN

THEY KEPT HER overnight in the hospital, and during that evening after dinner she overheard her nurse speaking Spanish with someone out in the hall. When her nurse came to check on her, she took advantage of the opportunity to speak Spanish. It was so much easier than speaking English. In reply to the nurse's routine inquiry about how she was feeling, Catalina said: *"Me siento bien. Estoy muy feliz."*

"Habla español?" the nurse said, looking surprised.

"Claro," she said. *"Es mi lengua materna."*

"I never would have guessed." The nurse paused as if she had detected something. "You know, I recognize your accent. You sound like a doctor in pediatrics."

"What's his name?"

"Dr. Rosenberg."

She sat up in bed. "David Rosenberg?"

"That's right. Do you know him?"

"I think I do." She couldn't believe it. "Do you know where he's from?"

"Argentina. And like you, he sounds like he's speaking Italian."

"Could you do me a favor? Could you tell him you have a patient named Catalina Rinaldi?"

"Okay. He's here during the day, and I have the night shift, so I won't see him. But I'll leave a note for him."

"Muchas gracias." She sat back against the pillow, marveling at the coincidence until she remembered that Dr. Rosenberg had done his residency at New York University Hospital, so it made sense for him to come back here.

The next morning, as she was in bed holding her baby, a man with a kindly face and intelligent eyes behind silver-rimmed glasses leaned into the doorway of her room and asked: "Catalina? Is it really you?"

"Yes," she said, glad to see him.

He came into the room and standing over her bedside asked: "*Qué te trae por aquí?*"

"It's a long story. Oh, by the way, this is Lucía."

"Hi, Lucía," the doctor said, inclining his head and smiling warmly. "You're a lovely girl."

"I had to leave Argentina," she told him.

"I can guess why. Did you ever get another residency?"

"No. I was on their list. So I worked full time in the *villa miseria*, at least until they bombed our clinic."

He gazed at her sadly. "What else did they do?"

"They killed my priest, they disappeared my father, they killed my friends, and they killed the father of Lucía. If I hadn't gotten out they would have killed me."

"I'm so sorry. I hope you got asylum here."

"I just got it, and I plan to stay."

"Where are you living?"

"In the East Village with my uncle and aunt. My uncle's father," she explained, retelling the family story, "came to America at the same time that my grandfather came to Argentina. They made a bet about who would do better."

"Right now it looks like your uncle's father won."

"It does," she agreed. "By the grace of God, they're here for me. I don't know what I would have done without them."

"What does your uncle do for a living?"

"He's a sculptor. He makes gigantic things out of metal for banks and corporations to install in the plazas and lobbies of their buildings. His name is Angelo Rinaldi."

"I think I've heard of him. What does your aunt do?"

"She's an artist, but she makes a living designing book covers for a publishing company."

"So now you're in the art world."

"Yeah, it's a different world."

"I live in a suburb on Long Island. It's good for my children.

They have excellent schools. And they already speak English like natives."

She figured that he had been here about a year and a half, and she was encouraged by his children adapting to a new country in that short time. "Well, I still have a long way to go before I speak English like a native."

He looked as if a thought was beginning to form in his mind. "So all you need is a residency to get your degree."

"That's right. I completed all the courses."

"To get a degree here you would have to transfer credits from there, and you might not get credit for everything. But based on my own experience, you probably wouldn't have to retake many courses. And once you completed all of them, you could then continue the residency you started with me. How does that sound?"

"It sounds wonderful."

"Then I can connect you with someone in admissions at the university who could help you with the transfer credits. But you should put that off for a while. Lucía should be your priority."

"Lucía *is* my priority," she said. "I'll call you when I'm ready."

He gave her a business card with his contact information, and then he left her, saying: "Take care."

Later that morning she was released from the hospital with her baby, and they were taken home by Angelo and Elda, who had a taxi waiting. In the weeks before her due date they had bought a crib and other essential items for a baby, so their apartment was ready for the addition to their family. And from then on Catalina organized her days to make Lucía her priority. Of course she got a lot of support from Elda and Angelo, who were so good, so loving with Lucía, she felt it was unfair that they couldn't have their own children. Whenever she thanked them for supporting her, they told her it was a blessing to have a baby in their home. They called Lucía their *nipotina*.

She waited until Lucía was almost a year old before she contacted Dr. Rosenberg, who put her in touch with a woman in admissions at New York University. Enabling her to meet with the woman,

Elda took a morning off from work to babysit Lucía, and Catalina walked to the university and somehow managed to find the office of admissions. There she was met by a receptionist, who made a phone call, and within a few minutes the woman she had talked with on the phone appeared. Her name was Ana Marino, and she was in her early thirties with short dark hair and serious dark eyes. Ana greeted her and led her through an open area where people were doing paperwork. She followed Ana into a small office, where she was offered the chair in front of a desk while Ana went around and sat in the chair behind it. After a preliminary conversation Ana said: "To get you started, we'll need an official transcript from your university."

Imagining what might happen if she requested a transcript from her university, Catalina asked: "What if I can not get one?"

Ana looked puzzled. "Why couldn't you get one?"

"The military government intervened my university, and they closed a lot of programs. They did not close the medical school, but they took over the administration, and as usual they have made a mess of things."

"Well, I don't know if we can give you credit for your courses there without an official transcript."

"You have other foreign students," she said, assuming she wasn't the only one, "who must have the same problem. So how do you solve it?"

"Sometimes we rely on unofficial transcripts, but only in special situations."

"Okay. Then I'll try to get an unofficial transcript."

"That would be helpful."

She believed that her mother might have records of her grades in the courses she had taken at the medical school. Her mother was good at recordkeeping, which she had done for the law firm as well as for the family. So it was a good possibility. "I will try to get the records for you."

"In the meantime, to move things along, you could tell me which courses you completed at your university."

"Okay. If you show me which courses you require, it will help me remember."

Ana picked up a printed sheet and handed it to her. "Check off the courses you completed, and when we get your records maybe we can give you credit for them."

She went down the list, which started with the biology courses she had taken during her first year and ended with the advanced courses she had taken during her fifth year. When she was done she had checked off all but four of the courses.

"That looks fine. How were your grades?"

"My grades were very good. In fact, I was in the top five percent of my class."

After a thoughtful silence Ana said: "If you don't mind my asking, why didn't you finish your degree there?"

"Because they would not let me."

"Who wouldn't let you?"

"The military government."

"But if you were such a good student—"

"They did not care about my grades. They only cared about my politics. And I was opposed to what they were doing, so I was on their list."

"You mean their shit list?"

She liked that expression. "Yes, their shit list."

"Well, I don't know anything about Argentina. I only know that my boss helped a doctor from Argentina get recertified. And that's why you were assigned to me."

Beginning to understand how things worked in New York, she was grateful for the referral from Dr. Rosenberg. She thanked Ana and told her she would let her know as soon as she had any records of the courses.

That evening she called her mother. It was more than two weeks since they had last talked so a phone call was due. She began talking about Lucía, and then she talked about other things until she asked her mother if she had any records from the medical school. She explained that she planned to complete her medical degree at New York University, and that she needed the records so that she could get credit for the courses she had taken at the University of Buenos Aires. Her mother thought she might have records but if she did they would be in boxes she hadn't yet unpacked, so she would have to look for them. Catalina was surprised that after living in Rio Cuarto for almost two years her mother still had boxes she hadn't unpacked, but she guessed they contained things that her mother didn't want to deal with. They left it that her mother would go through the boxes and would let her know if she found any records.

A week later her mother called her and told her she had found records of her grades all the way back to elementary school. They discussed how her mother should send the records, and not trusting the mail system they agreed that her mother should give them to a friend travelling to New York on business. At the moment her mother didn't know anyone who was planning such a trip, but no matter how long they had to wait for someone who was, it would still be more reliable than the mail, and it would probably get the records to Catalina sooner. Relieved that her mother had found the records, she was willing to wait as long as necessary because the last thing she wanted to do was take all those courses again.

Six weeks later the records were brought from Rio Cuarto by a man who came to New York to get a bank loan for his business. The man, whom her mother had known since high school, was nice enough to come to the East Village and give the records to her personally, and she thanked him with all her heart.

Her courses from the medical school were accepted in transfer, so in the spring semester she started taking one of the four courses she was missing. If she did well in this course, she planned to increase her course load in the fall semester, by which time she would have a better command of English. Meanwhile, Elda took time off from work to be with Lucía while Catalina was in class or in the library studying.

She did well in the course, so she registered for two courses in the fall semester. She also did well in those courses, and after she completed the last course in the spring semester Dr. Rosenberg resumed mentoring her in a residency. She learned a lot from working with him, and at times she wondered what might have happened to them if their relationship hadn't been interrupted more than three years ago. But knowing what did happen to them she felt they were lucky to be in New York, away from the turmoil of their country.

When she finally got her license as a physician her uncle and aunt had a party for her at their apartment to which they invited several friends as well as Dr. Rosenberg, who renewed his brief acquaintance with Lucía. By then Lucía was almost five years old, a happy child, and when he introduced himself to her she acted as if she remembered meeting him the day after she was born. And having a daughter, he easily related to her.

A few weeks later Catalina began working at Dr. Rosenberg's pediatrics clinic, which was near the hospital. She had treated children in the *villas*, but now she could help her patients so much more than she could then. She had more training, and she also had the experience of having a child of her own. By then there were two beds in her room, and though it was a little tight she and Lucía didn't get in each other's way too often. At times she wondered if they should have their own apartment, but she knew how much her uncle and her aunt liked having them there, and with all the uncertainty in the world she liked living in a family where she and Lucía were blessed with love.

From her regular phone conversations with her mother she heard that the situation in Argentina was deteriorating, and that the military were going to extremes to stay in power, even to the point of invading the islands that belonged to Britain but were claimed by Argentina, arousing the fervent patriotism of people who had learned in school to proclaim: "LAS MALVINAS SON ARGENTINAS!" The war proved to be a disaster, but the good thing about the humiliating defeat was that it caused the demise of the military, who finally handed over power to civilians. When Raúl Alfonsín was elected president just three weeks after Lucía's sixth birthday Catalina decided that it would be safe to visit Argentina to see her mother and her brother, to see any friends who might have survived, and to show Lucía where she had come from.

Lucía was in first grade at the neighborhood elementary school, so they could go to Argentina either during the holiday break or they could wait until June when school was over. If they went in December it would be summer in Argentina, and at least for a while they would escape from the cold weather. If they waited until June it would be winter in Argentina, but they could stay there longer. Deciding not to wait, she booked the flights on dates that expanded the break period at both ends, so that they would have three weeks in Argentina.

Catalina was now a U.S. citizen, but she still felt a twinge of fear at the thought of going back to Argentina. Though the military were no longer in power, the police could arrest her for being involved in a kidnapping, which was a crime under any type of government. She subdued this fear by reminding herself that they would be looking for a woman with black hair and the name of Martina Aguirre, but she couldn't make it go away.

Their flight departed at nine in the evening several days before Christmas. Knowing how long the flight was, Catalina had brought a tablet of paper, crayons, and a few children's books for Lucía to pass the time with. She let Lucía have the window seat, where the girl could look out and watch what was happening as the plane slowly backed out of the gate. Lucía leaned against her and held her hand during the takeoff, and once the plane had leveled off she got the tablet and started drawing pictures. The food was as bad as Catalina remembered, but Lucía liked the lemon cake and asked for her untouched piece as well. Luckily, she found a movie that Lucía could watch, and that killed time. By midnight Lucía was finally sleeping, with a blanket pulled up to her neck. Catalina turned out her light and tried to sleep, but she kept imagining a scene at the airport in which she was arrested.

The plane landed with a bump around ten in the morning, and they staggered up the ramp into the terminal. As they lined up for immigration she prayed that nothing would go wrong. They were in the line for nonresidents, which she felt should be safe, but as people used to say, in Argentina if something could go wrong it would go wrong. And praying that nothing would go wrong, she slid their U.S. passports across the counter toward the official.

"You're Americans?" he said in English.

"Yes. We are," she said simply.

"Mother and daughter?"

She nodded. "Yes."

"What is the purpose of your visit?"

"To see my mother and her grandmother."

"How long do you plan to stay?"

"For three weeks." She had noticed that like many Argentines he spoke with a British accent, which she used to have before it evolved into a New York accent.

"Welcome to Argentina," he said, stamping their passports.

With a prayer of thanks she guided Lucía to the baggage area.

For their flight to Rio Cuarto they had to go to the Aeroparque Jorge Newbery, which was in the city, so as soon as they had retrieved their suitcases she found a taxi to take them there. On the way they passed the *colectivo* stop from which she had walked to the *quinta*, and for her that was the worst part of the trip. She must have shown her feelings because Lucía asked her if she was all right. She reassured Lucía, saying it was only a momentary fit of exhaustion.

The flight from Buenos Aires to Rio Cuarto took about an hour and a half, and when they disembarked she saw her mother and brother waiting for them. It was almost seven years since she had seen her mother, and bursting into tears she rushed to her mother, pulling Lucía along with her. She buried herself in her mother's arms, sobbing with relief and giving thanks for their reunion.

After a while she drew back her head and gazed at her mother, noticing that her mother looked a bit older, with streaks of gray in her dark hair, and then she introduced Lucía, saying: "*Mamá, esta es Lucía, mi regalo de Dios. Lucía, esta es tu abuela.*"

"Hey, ladies," Marco said. "What about me?"

She turned to her brother and realized that he was the one who had changed the most. The last time she saw him Marco was a kid, and now he was a grown man. Of course she had learned from the phone calls with her mother that Marco was married and had two young children, so she shouldn't have been surprised by the change, but in her mind he had still been a kid.

She hugged Marco and introduced him to Lucía, who asked him if he was really her uncle. He told her that he really was, and Lucía rewarded him with a kiss.

They retrieved their suitcases and loaded them into Marco's car, a spacious old Rambler like the car their father had owned, and Marco drove them from the airport into town. Catalina had come to Rio Cuarto many times on visits with her mother to see her grandparents and her uncle, and she recognized buildings, the main plaza, and finally the house where her mother had grown up and now lived with Marco, his wife, and their children. The house had been in their family for three generations, and though it wasn't grand, it had five bedrooms and two full bathrooms, so it could accommodate all of them including guests.

Marco's wife, whose name was Beatriz, was waiting for them in front of the house. She was a solid woman, and she greeted Catalina with a potent hug. She kissed Lucía on top of her head, and then she led them into the house and upstairs to their room, followed by Marco with their suitcases. It was early afternoon, and she suggested that they might want to take a *siesta* to recover from their trip, explaining that it was customary for people in Rio Cuarto to retire during the mid-day heat. Catalina liked the idea, and so did Lucía, and even though they each had a twin bed, they flopped together on the same bed and drifted into sleep.

When they got up they took showers and put on clean clothes and went downstairs, where they found Marco and Beatriz in back of the house on the patio, playing with their children. Santino, the boy, was four, and he looked like his mother. Emma, the girl, was two, and she looked like her father. After a while Catalina's mother joined them and took the children away to feed them dinner. At that point Marco offered her a *gin y tónica*, which she accepted, and he got a Fanta orange for Lucía. Their conversation began with generalities and then became more specific after Catalina asked Marco about the family business, which provided rentals and maintenance of agricultural equipment. Their mother's brother, who had run the business for many years, was in the process of retiring and handing it over to Marco, who was hopeful about its prospects now that the military were no longer in power.

"They didn't know how to manage the economy," he told her. "They didn't even know how to fight a war. So what good were they?"

"I don't know," she said. "Are they really gone now?"

"They're gone from the government. They're still behind the scenes, but they don't have the influence they used to have. I mean, people don't trust them anymore."

"You think they'll ever return to power?"

Marco shook his head. "No, I don't think so. After the disaster in the Malvinas, people have no respect for them."

She was glad to hear that. She could even imagine coming back to live in Argentina.

Her mother rejoined them after Beatriz took the children off to bed, and Marco began to prepare steaks on an outdoor grill. Beatriz brought a bowl of mixed green salad, which they ate at a table on the patio. Marco served the steaks with potatoes he had roasted on the grill, and they stopped talking long enough to dig into the food.

They lingered after dinner until it was time for Lucía to go to bed. Catalina took her upstairs and got her settled, with a blanket positioned at the foot of the bed in case it was needed later. Kissing her daughter goodnight, she asked: "How do you like Argentina?"

"I like it fine," Lucía said. "But I miss my *nonna* and my *nonno*."

"Yeah, I know. It would be nice if we could all be together in the same place."

She sat on the other bed until Lucía had fallen asleep, and then she went downstairs and out to the patio, where she found her mother, Marco, and Beatriz.

It wasn't long before she became the main topic of their conversation. They asked her questions about her life in America, and in answering them she learned things about herself that might not have otherwise come to her attention. Among other things, she learned how much her identity depended on her being a mother, a doctor, and a refugee. She realized how much she had changed from what she had been in Argentina.

She and her mother remained on the patio after Marco and Beatriz had gone to bed. By now they were sipping sambuca and feeling mellow.

"While I was listening to you," her mother told her, "I was reminded of how I felt when I left Rio Cuarto and went to Buenos Aires. I could have stayed here and gotten married and lived a very comfortable life. But I wanted something different, and please don't laugh, but I was inspired by Eva Perón."

"Eva Perón?" Catalina was surprised. Of course her father had been a Peronist, at least before Perón revealed himself as a fascist, but she never imagined that her mother was inspired by Eva. "In what way?"

"Well, she was a girl from a province who went to Buenos Aires and made it. I didn't grow up poor like her, but I felt I had limited opportunities in Rio Cuarto, so I went off to Buenos Aires and enrolled in a secretarial school, which led to a job at your father's law firm, which led to what happened in my life."

"I hope you're not saying what happens in our lives depends on who we marry."

"In my case it did. And if Eva hadn't married Juan Perón, we might have never heard of her."

"But a woman can achieve things without being married."

"Of course," her mother said.. "A lot of women, including you, have achieved things without being married."

"So how do you feel about Eva now?"

"I still admire her. She wasn't a saint, but she was the best thing about Perón. She sincerely wanted to help the poor, and when he lost her, Perón didn't care about the poor anymore."

"I care about the poor. And I'm not a saint. In fact—" She hesitated, wondering if she should say it, and then she blurted out: "I'm a sinner."

"If you mean having sex without being married, forget about it. Look at the beautiful child you have."

"I don't mean that. I did something that was really bad."

"You know," her mother said with a look of understanding, "in our phone conversations I had a feeling you had something on your conscience, but I never asked you what it was because I could tell you didn't want to talk about it."

"Well, I want to talk about it now."

"All right," her mother said. "Tell me about it."

Opening her heart, she told her mother everything, and her mother listened closely.

When she had finished, her mother said: "You did do something that was really bad, but you're sorry for it, so God has forgiven you. Now you have to forgive yourself."

"I can't forgive myself."

"Why can't you?"

Pierced by her feeling of guilt, she said: "Because I'm responsible for the deaths of my friends and Lucía's father."

"You didn't kill them, the military did."

"But I gave the military a reason for killing them."

"The military didn't need a reason for killing them. They killed them because they were trained to kill people."

She considered this. "It wasn't in their nature to kill people?"

"No. It wasn't. God didn't create them to kill people. They had to be trained to kill people. So what we have to do," her mother said, "is forgive the military."

"I can't forgive them. Can you forgive them?"

"I think I can. At least I don't hate them as much as I did. And most of the time I feel blessed to have my children and my grandchildren."

"I feel blessed to have Lucía."

"Well, that's a start."

That night, as she lay in bed awake, she pondered what her mother had said, especially about having to forgive the military. That was what Father Francisco kept saying in their conversations. It kept coming up, over and over. But for all the good things that were happening in her life, she wasn't getting any closer to forgiving the people who had killed her priest, her father, her friends, and Lucio.

They celebrated Christmas by going to Mass at Nuestra Señora del Carmen and having a feast on the patio, joined by Beatriz's parents. By now Catalina was used to Christmas in the winter, so she had to readapt herself to Christmas in the summer. She also had to explain to Lucía that children in Argentina didn't get presents on Christmas but on Reyes when the Three Kings visited the baby Jesus. She planned to buy presents for Lucía on her trip to Buenos Aires, which she had scheduled for two days after New Year's. She was going there by herself because she believed that Lucía would have a better time in Rio Cuarto with her grandmother, her uncle and aunt, and her young cousins.

She had a morning flight, and she was met by Mercedes at the airport. Mercedes, who looked exactly the same as she remembered, advanced toward her and embraced her, making her realize how much she had missed her role model. She had brought only carry-on luggage, so they went directly to the lot where Mercedes had parked her jeep.

"*No me lo digas*," she said. "Is this the same jeep?"

"Yes, it is. My mechanic takes good care of it."

As they drove out of the airport Mercedes said: "Before I take you home, would you like to see what's happening in the *villa?*"

"*Claro que sí.* So what's happening?"

"We're rebuilding the clinic, the church, and the school."

"That's wonderful. When will they be finished?"

"By early March. In time for the next school year."

"I assume you have teachers lined up."

"Oh, yes. We do. We even have a Sister of Mercy to whip them into shape."

"What about the clinic?"

"I have a medical student helping me. She's very good, though not as good as you were."

"I really didn't know anything."

"If that's how you feel," Mercedes said, "you must have learned a lot since then."

"I have," she said. "I have a good mentor. I've always had good mentors."

They drove from the airport through Palermo, Villa Crespo, Caballito, and finally Flores, which brought back memories. She was struck by how little she had known of the world back then, and she felt a pang of empathy for that innocent girl.

Mercedes parked her jeep at the edge of the *villa*, near the café where they had meetings, and led her through streets that looked no better than before. When they came to where the church had been she saw the walls of concrete block risen to the level of her shoulders.

"We have a priest," Mercedes told her. "A young man who was inspired by Father Francisco to serve the poor."

"God bless Father Francisco," she said. "Are there many of his followers left?"

"There are. He had a lot of followers, and most of them have survived. Remember Orlando?"

"The orthopedics guy?"

"Right. He has a practice in Flores now, and he's going to help us when we have to deal with broken bones."

They went on to the clinic, which was further along than the church. She could see that it would be bigger than the previous clinic. "So how are you going to staff it?"

"We're going to have two doctors, two residents, and two nurses. Of course I'll be one of the doctors."

"Do you have the other doctor?"

"No. We're still looking. We want her to be the right person."

"You're going to have two female doctors?"

"We're hoping to," Mercedes said. "We'll have at least one male resident for the guys who don't trust female doctors."

Last, they went and looked at the school, which was further along than the clinic. Mercedes stressed the urgency of having the building finished in time for the beginning of the school year. It would be large enough to accommodate the seven compulsory grades of elementary school.

Impressed by the buildings, Catalina asked: "Where did all the money come from?"

"It mostly came from private donors. We got a big grant from a nonprofit organization that has funding from an American charity. And we got money from the church."

"Anything from the government?"

"No. But I'm hopeful. At least this government says it wants to help the poor."

"Speaking of money, I brought the money I owe you for my plane ticket."

Mercedes shook her head, saying: "You don't owe me money. But if you want to, you could make a donation to our project."

"I want to," she said. "I want to be a regular donor."

"*Gracias*. Well, let's go and have lunch."

They went to the café, where they had sandwiches of ham and cheese, and then Mercedes drove them home.

That evening, while they were having dinner, Mercedes offered her a full-time position at her clinic in Almagro and a part-time position as one of the two doctors at the clinic in the *villa*. Since it was a big decision for her, Mercedes suggested that she sleep on it during the two nights she planned to stay.

Catalina put off thinking about it while she did other things, which included a visit to the cemetery where Father Francisco was buried and a visit to the church where they had recently placed a plaque on an outer wall to honor him. She also went to Caballito and saw Lucio's parents, whom Mercedes had helped her to locate. When she showed them a picture of their granddaughter she wished she had brought Lucía with her, and she promised to bring her the next time she visited them. And finally she had lunch with Olivia, who was working at a clinic in Belgrano. As they talked about their different lives she reflected on how their paths had diverged with her decision to follow Father Francisco, and since Olivia had a husband and two children as well as her position at the clinic Catalina was glad that her friend had decided not to follow Father Francisco.

On the way to the airport for her flight back to Rio Cuarto she asked Mercedes to give her more time to think about her offer because she expected that her mother would want her to come back to Argentina and live with her family. Mercedes said she understood, and she told her to take as much time as she needed to make a decision.

She had found time to go to a bookstore in the city center and buy several children's books for Lucía, who loved books, and she gave them to Lucía as presents for Reyes. Along with presents from her grandmother and her uncle and her aunt, Lucía had a lot of presents to open on Reyes, and she happily commented that it was even better than Christmas. Beatriz had bought a Rosca de Reyes, a ring-shaped cake, which Lucía joined Santino and Emma in polishing off.

The next day she stayed up late talking with her mother, who proposed that she come back to Argentina and live with them in Rio Cuarto, which needed another pediatrician. Her mother had even checked with a clinic and identified a specific position. She told her mother that she had been offered a position in Buenos Aires, where she could pursue her mission of helping the poor. Her mother pointed out that there was poverty in Rio Cuarto, so she could pursue her mission there. After the years of separation and exile, she was tempted by the prospect of living in a reunited family, and she told her mother she would think about it.

She lay awake most of the night thinking about it, torn between the pull of her role model and the pull of her mother. She found her way out of this tug-of-war by considering the needs of Lucía, who was young enough to adapt to Argentina but would have a wider range of opportunities in America. On top of that she remembered all that Angelo and Elda had done for her, and how they would feel if their *nipotina* was taken away to the ends of the earth. Her mother lived in a house with her son, her daughter-in-law, and her grandchildren, but Angelo and Elda would have no family if she came back to Argentina. And she considered her own needs, which included the opportunity to pursue her mission as well as the security she had found in America, where she would never have to worry about the military returning to power. After weighing the needs of others and herself, she decided to remain in America.

TWELVE

AS SHE WATCHED her daughter grow and develop over the next few years Catalina was glad that she had decided not to go back to Argentina. Lucía was thriving, she was doing well at school, and she had a lot of friends. At home she preferred reading to watching television, and with Elda as her teacher she learned to draw, revealing a talent for capturing the essence of human faces. Above all, she was a happy child, a loving child, attached to her mother, her *nonna*, and her *nonno*.

When Lucía was almost nine the apartment across the hall became available, presenting the opportunity to expand their living space without moving, so with the blessing of her uncle and aunt Catalina rented it. Lucía could now have her own room, which would be good for her development, and their family would still be physically intact. They still ate dinner together, though now Catalina could at times contribute by cooking in her own kitchen and bringing food across the hall.

Every year after school was out in June they went to Argentina and spent about a month there, experiencing winter in the middle of the American summer. Lucía always got involved in helping her aunt with her two young cousins, acting like their older sister, and Catalina always went to Buenos Aires for a few days to stay with Mercedes and follow the progress of her mission in the *villa*. She always noticed some positive changes in the *villa*, though it still had a long way to go before most people had indoor plumbing and potable water.

Lucía was beginning her freshman year in high school when Dr. Rosenberg decided to concentrate his practice on Long Island, where he lived and already had an office. He invited Catalina to join him there, but it would have required commuting or moving, and she didn't want to disrupt Lucía at a time when it was so important for her to have continuity in her life, so Catalina declined the offer and began a training program for a specialty in internal medicine. By the time Lucía began her senior year of high school Catalina had received board certification for that specialty.

In the meantime she became an active member of a community group that Elda had started with a friend who lived on the second floor of their building. The friend's name was Rachel, and she owned a literary agency which she claimed was the only remaining leftist agency in the city. She invited Catalina to her apartment, which was dominated by piles of books. She told Catalina to take as many books as she wanted because they were impossible to get rid of. While they had coffee, sitting in a living room strewn with book proposals, Rachel expounded on the virtues of Angelo and Elda, who in her opinion were the most amazing people in the world. It was hard to believe they were in their eighties.

The purpose of the community group was to help the poor in the neighborhood and to prevent them from being driven out by gentrification. Rachel, who was Jewish, introduced her to the Catholic Worker, which planted a seed that eventually grew into a vision of the practice Catalina hoped to establish. Its mission would be to serve the neighborhood with a focus on the poor. Of course it took money to establish a practice, and she still had student loans to pay, but with the guarantee of Angelo and Elda she managed to get a loan from their bank, and she opened her office in June of the year when Lucía graduated from high school. Lucía had applied to several colleges, including St. Catherine in Yonkers and Mount St. Vincent in the Bronx, but she decided to go to Hunter College in Manhattan, which had three advantages over the other colleges: it had a wider range of programs, it was closer, and it was less expensive.

Lucía was undecided about her major with the possibilities ranging from a pre-med program to an art history program, and she ended up majoring in English because she liked reading and she believed that this major would provide a good base for any profession she decided to pursue. For a while she didn't rule out being a doctor, but in her junior year she decided to become a teacher at the elementary school level, which made a lot of sense because as a babysitter in the neighborhood she had demonstrated a natural ability to relate to children. And she decided to stay at Hunter for graduate school.

By then her *nonna* and *nonno* were finally showing signs of age, and they lived long enough to see their *nipotina* get her master's degree in education. Neither of them had a major health problem, but they reached the point where their bodies simply wore out. Angelo died in early June right after Lucía's graduation, and Elda died two months later. Their deaths were devastating for Lucía who hadn't lost anyone to death before, and the only thing that roused her from the depths of grief was the fact that she had a job with an elementary school in Yonkers and she was embarking on her career.

Catalina helped her find an apartment in Yonkers and helped her furnish it, but she had mixed feelings about her daughter leaving home. On the one hand she felt that it was good for a young woman of Lucía's age to separate from her mother, but on the other hand she missed the person who had been the center of her life for twenty-four years. She compensated by throwing herself into her practice, but that didn't fill the emptiness resulting from the deaths of Angelo and Elda and the departure of Lucía.

She went to Mass alone on Sunday, and she stopped at the church every day on her way to work. Though the guilt over her role in the kidnapping of Colonel Yribarren had sunk below her conscious mind during the years of raising a child and establishing a practice, it had never gone away, and now that she was less occupied with family matters it rose to the surface like a monster that was only biding its time and waiting for an opportunity to attack. So the main purpose of her daily visits to the church was to keep the monster at bay.

One morning when she turned in the aisle to leave the church after genuflecting she saw a priest standing behind the last pew. It wasn't the parish priest, it was someone she had never seen before, and as she approached him she noticed that he had brown skin and indigenous features like the people she had known in the *villas*.

Stopping in front of him she said: "Hi, father. How are you doing?"

"I'm doing okay," he said with a pleasant smile. "How about you? I have a feeling you have something on your mind."

He spoke English with a familiar foreign accent, so she replied in Spanish, saying: "*Sí, hay algo que me preocupa.*"

"*¿Quieres contármelo?*"

"I don't have time to make a confession. I have to go to work."

"What kind of work do you do?"

"I'm a doctor. I have a practice in this neighborhood." Before he could ask another question she said: "I haven't seen you here before."

"I have just been assigned here as assistant pastor."

"Where are you from?"

"El Salvador. I was born and raised there, but I came here with my family when I was fifteen. We were refugees."

"I understand. I came here as a refugee."

"Where are you from?"

"Argentina."

He shook his head sadly. "I heard about your war there. It was like the war we had in El Salvador."

Acting on instinct she asked: "Are you free this evening?"

"You mean for confession?"

"No. For dinner. I usually leave my office around six. I could come here then and take you to a local restaurant."

"That would be nice. I'll see you then."

"What's your name?"

"Benicio Suárez."

"My name is Catalina Rinaldi."

With a smile he said: "Is everyone from Argentina Italian?"

"Almost everyone," she said, smiling back at him.

She took him to the Peruvian chicken restaurant where she knew they would get a good meal. As they talked she realized how much they had in common beginning with the fact that they were both refugees from wars between military governments and people fighting for social justice. They talked about Óscar Romero, the archbishop in El Salvador who was assassinated for his support of the common people, just as Father Francisco was assassinated for his support of the common people. She knew that the cause for beatification of Archbishop Romero had been initiated by Pope John Paul II, and she liked to think that a similar cause would be initiated for Father Francisco.

They were still talking when they left the restaurant, so she took Father Benicio to a nearby coffee shop where they continued talking. At one point after reviewing what they had in common she finally said: "But in one way we're different as refugees."

"How are we different?"

"You're innocent, and I'm guilty."

"Guilty of what?"

"Committing a crime, a mortal sin, which led to the deaths of other people."

He looked at her with empathy. "You want to tell me about it now, or would you rather tell me about it in a confession?"

"I want to tell you about it now if you have the time."

"I have the time."

So she told him the whole story, beginning with her decision to follow Father Francisco and ending with the massacre of her friends and Lucio.

When she had finished he said: "Okay. You're guilty of a major crime, a mortal sin. But that was twenty-five years ago, and by now you must know that God has forgiven you."

"I hope he has. But I haven't forgiven myself."

"I see." He looked at her with a glimmer in his eyes. "So you don't come to church to ask God to forgive you."

"No. I come to church to ask God to help me forgive myself."

"Well, isn't that being arrogant?"

"How do you mean?"

"I mean putting yourself above God by not being willing to do something that God has already done for you."

"I'm willing," she said, "but I'm not able."

"You'll be able to forgive yourself as soon as you forgive the military for what they did to your priest, your father, your friends, and the father of your child."

"That's what Father Francisco tells me."

"Tells you?" he asked with a puzzled look.

"I have conversations with him," she explained. "We go back and forth, and we always end with him telling me that."

"So why don't you do what he tells you to do?"

"Because I can't. I just can't."

After a silence the priest said: "I assume you realize that if you're having conversations with Father Francisco, what he tells you is coming from your own heart."

"I guess it is. I never thought of it that way."

"So listen to your heart," he said, "and do what your heart tells you to do."

"Okay. I'll try. It might help if I come to you for confession."

"It might. At least it won't hurt."

She left him at the church and from there she walked home, pondering what he had said and wondering how she could put his advice into action.

A few days later she made a formal confession to Father Benicio. He must have thought about what she had told him in the coffee shop because he was ready with a penance: he told her to pray for the soul of Colonel Yribarren, and to pray for his family.

She understood the purpose of this, and from then on when she stopped at the church on her way to work she tried to carry out the penance. She was able to pray for the soul of the colonel because she had known him, and there had been some kind of relationship between them. But she had trouble praying for his family because she didn't know anything about them. She knew that the colonel lived alone in an apartment, but she didn't know if he had a family. Was he married? Did he have children? If only she knew something about them, she might be able to pray for them, but they completely eluded her.

One evening she had dinner with Rachel, whom she met at the Peruvian chicken restaurant. Rachel was happy because she had just sold a book by a young upcoming socialist, and she was hoping it would convert at least some people to the idea of a political program for social justice, though she admitted that it wasn't such a good time for socialists.

While they ate their chicken, rice, and beans Catalina shared with Rachel her experience with the new assistant pastor of her church.

"His family were refugees from El Salvador," she told Rachel. "So he understands."

"My family were refugees from Ukraine," Rachel said.

"Was there a civil war there?"

"No. But there were pogroms to get rid of Jews. They didn't have the modern techniques of the Nazis, but they were effective all the same."

"I can imagine," she said, based on her own experience.

"Anyway, what's his name?"

"The new priest? His name is Benicio Suárez, and I brought him here for dinner. And then I took him to our coffee shop, where I told him what I did in Argentina."

"What did he say?"

"He said that God has forgiven me."

"So he agrees with all the people who know you."

"I told him I haven't forgiven myself, and he said I was putting myself above God by not being willing to do something that God has already done for me."

"I agree with him," Rachel said. "If God has forgiven you, who do you think you are that you haven't forgiven yourself?"

"I'm willing to forgive myself, but I'm not able to."

"You mean you just can't?"

"Yeah. I just can't. But Father Benicio told me I'll be able to as soon as I forgive the military for what they did to my priest, my father, my friends, and the father of my child."

"Well, I can see how that wouldn't be easy. I mean, I can't forgive the Nazis for what they did to us."

"Our military was evil, but they weren't as evil as the Nazis."

"Evil is evil. It's all the same."

They paused while the waiter asked if they would like a dessert. They usually didn't have one, but to buy some more time at the restaurant they ordered a flan with two spoons.

"I made a formal confession to him," Catalina continued. "And you know what penance he gave me? He told me to pray for the soul of the colonel and to pray for his family."

"Have you done that?"

"I've prayed for the soul of the colonel, but I haven't been able to pray for his family because I have no idea who they are."

"You mean you don't know if he had a wife and children?"

"No. I only know he ordered the torture and execution of more than twenty prisoners."

"So he was evil," Rachel said. "But evil men have families."

"I know. And they could be living in Argentina, unable to forgive the guerrillas who killed their husband or father."

"Or grandfather. If he were alive he'd be my age, wouldn't he?"

"I guess he would be. And his grandchildren would be Lucía's age. Whoever they are, I keep trying to imagine them, and I keep trying to pray for them, but I'm not getting anywhere."

"So ask your priest to give you another penance."

Catalina laughed. "I can't do that."

"Why can't you? If the penance isn't working for you, then try something else."

"It isn't like therapy."

"I think it is. I mean, isn't religion a form of therapy?"

"In a sense I guess it is, but it's more than that. It gives us a vision of something beyond the material world."

"Yeah, I know. But in the meantime we're here in the material world, and we have to make it a better place."

"I know we do." She paused to reflect. "You think that should be enough for me?"

"I think it should," Rachel said, picking up a spoon to taste the flan that the waiter had set down on their table. "Mm, this is good. You gotta try it before I eat it all."

Two months later she was standing in front of her building, waiting for the guy to make the next move. She was ready for him to take out a gun and shoot her, or take out a knife and stab her. But instead he said: "Before I kill you, I want you to know why."

She searched his face, realizing that he was only in his mid-twenties, about the same age as Lucía, no longer a kid but not yet an adult. "Okay. Tell me why you want to kill me."

"I can't tell you here. Is there a place where we can go?"

After completely ruling out the possibility of letting this guy into her apartment, Catalina said: "Yeah. There's a coffee shop around the corner."

"That sounds fine. But don't try anything," he warned her, patting the right pocket of his pants which bulged presumably with a gun.

They walked in silence to the coffee shop where she had first told Father Benicio about her sin. Inside, she led the guy to a corner table and they sat down. Absurdly, she asked him what he would like to drink, and he said an espresso. She signaled the girl who waited on tables and ordered two espressos.

After the girl had brought the espressos Catalina said: "You told me you're the grandson of Colonel Yribarren. What's your name?"

"Ricardo Morales."

"How did you find me?"

"It wasn't easy. You didn't leave a trail. But I finally got access to military records, and I found you on a list."

"How did you get access to military records?"

"I was studying law," Ricardo told her, "and I managed to get a position on a team of lawyers who were defending the military."

She knew about the trials having learned from her mother that the civilian government was prosecuting selected military officers for war crimes. "So you found me on a list. But how did you tie me to your grandfather?"

"I investigated. I went to the club where he was lured away by a girl named Martina Aguirre. I went to the hotel where he was abducted. I went to the *quinta* where he was held for ransom. I learned from a nearby *villa miseria* that a doctor from the *quinta* was providing medical services for them. I got access to the records of the medical school, and I didn't find Martina Aguirre, but I found a student whose residency was interrupted because she was on the military's list. She transferred her credits to New York University and became a resident under a doctor from Argentina who was also on the military's list. In fact, it was the same doctor who had been her mentor in Argentina. So I decided that Martina Aguirre must be you."

"Martina Aguirre *is* me," Catalina admitted, impressed by the diligence of the young man's investigation. "I was the girl who lured your grandfather away from the club."

"I know why you did it. You needed money. So you did what the Montoneros were doing to get money. But why did you pick my grandfather?"

"Do you really want to know?"

"Yes." Ricardo met her gaze with his young brown eyes. "I really want to know."

"Your grandfather, Colonel Yribarren, was in charge of a unit that was transporting Montonero prisoners, and he gave an order to torture and execute them."

"I don't believe it."

"Well, it's true," she said. "So you should have expanded your investigation."

"I couldn't do that. I was on a team of lawyers who were defending the military. But even if what you said is true, it doesn't justify what you did."

"You're right. It doesn't."

After a long silence he said: "In case you're wondering why I want justice, you have to understand how your crime affected my family. My mother was the daughter of Colonel Yribarren, his only child, and she was very close to him. She was two months pregnant when you kidnapped him and killed him, and she was never the same again."

"I'm sorry," she said, feeling his pain.

"After I was born she went into a severe depression, and she never recovered. I can still remember lying awake at night and hearing her cry. I wanted to help her, to relieve her sorrow, but nothing I could say or do made her feel better. When I was seven she killed herself, and I felt it was my fault for failing to help her."

"I'm so sorry," she said, taking his hand and holding it.

"There's no way I'll ever have peace. But at least I can have justice."

"If you kill me, you'll have justice," she said, "but that won't do anything for you. In fact, it will ruin your life."

"My life is already ruined," he said. "I dropped out of the university to find you."

"You can go back to the university, but if you kill me you can't go back."

"I don't care. I have nothing to go back to."

"Listen," she told him, taking his other hand as well. "The military killed my priest and disappeared my father, so I believed it would be justice to kidnap your grandfather, especially after what he did to those Montonero prisoners. But the kidnapping led to the deaths of my friends and the father of my child, so I feel responsible for their deaths. In fact, I've spent my whole life trying to forgive myself for helping to kidnap your grandfather, and I don't want you to spend your whole life trying to forgive yourself for killing me."

"Why do you care about me?"

"I care because I understand why you want to kill me. And let me show you something," she said, letting go of his hands and opening her pocketbook. She got out her wallet and found the picture of Lucía that was taken for the school where she was teaching. She handed the picture to Ricardo, saying: "This is my daughter, my only child. Her name is Lucía. Her father was killed by the military."

Ricardo silently gazed at the picture.

"She's probably around the age of your mother when her father was killed. So remember what his death did to her, and think about what my death would do to my daughter."

Ricardo continued gazing at the picture while his eyes slowly filled with tears.

"If you still want justice, go ahead and kill me. But you don't need justice, and I didn't need it when I helped to kidnap your grandfather. What you need, and what I needed, is mercy."

Without a word Ricardo handed the picture back to her and rose from the table.

"Where are you going?" she asked him.

"Back to Argentina." He offered his hand to her. "*Paz, señora.*"

"*Paz, señor,*" she said, clasping his hand tightly.

On her way home she stopped at the church, which was still open, and she thanked God for the outcome of her meeting with Ricardo. And then she went home, where there was a phone message from her daughter.

Lucía answered after one ring as if she was expecting the call.

"Hey, where were you?" Lucía asked. "Out on a date?"

"No, not exactly. So how did things go with your dinner?"

"Fine. He liked the pasta. He said it was almost as good as his mother makes."

"Well, that's the ultimate compliment."

"Yeah." Lucía paused. "He's going to the DR this weekend. He asked me to go with him so I can meet his grandparents."

"Are you going with him?"

"No. I think it's too soon for me to meet his grandparents. You know what I mean?"

"Yeah, I know." She was very glad that Lucía was taking her time with the relationship.

"With school out, I don't have much to do, so I wondered if I could come and stay with you for a few days."

"*Claro que sí.* Why don't you come on Friday? We'll have the weekend, and I'll reschedule my appointments for next week so we can have more time together."

"That would be great. Are you all right?" Lucía asked as if she had detected something.

"Yeah, I'm all right. I just feel like taking a break."

"You hardly ever take one. You should have been a teacher, *viste?* You'd have most of the summer off."

"I should have been a shrink," she said, reflecting on how she had turned around the colonel's grandson. "I'd have the month of August off."

"So I'll see you on Friday. When's your last appointment?"

"I don't remember. But be at my office around six. We can go to the local Argentine restaurant."

"*Ah, maravilloso! Podemos tener palmitos con salsa golf?*"

"*Claro. Y bifes de chorizo con papas fritas.*"

"*Te amo, mamá.*"

"*Yo también te amo, hija.*"

Later, in bed, she prayed for Ricardo, and in the process she found the way that would lead to forgiving the military. And that night she slept more peacefully than she had since her decision to play a role in the kidnapping.

Introduction

As she is leaving for work one morning Catalina Rinaldi confronts a young man standing on the sidewalk in front of her apartment building in New York City, and he addresses her with the alias she used in a crime against the military government in Argentina many years ago. She is startled by the encounter, especially since the guy speaks English with the accent of someone from Argentina, but she recovers enough to deny that she's the person he thinks she is, and she walks away, wondering if he's an Argentine police agent who has managed to track her and finally find her. She can get away from him during the day, but he knows where she lives, and she can expect him to be waiting outside her building that evening when she goes home. So what does this guy want from her? Does he want to arrest her and take her back to Argentina where she will be justly punished for her crime? Does he want revenge? She can only imagine, and she can't ask for police protection because if she does, it will all come out: what she did in Argentina and its fatal consequences. Although it was dormant, her feeling of guilt was always alive in the bottom of her heart, and now it has been aroused by a guy identifying her as the woman who lured a man to his death, which led to the deaths of other people, including the father of her child.

Catalina was born and raised in the Flores neighborhood of Buenos Aires. Her father was a lawyer with a mission to serve the working class, and during the time when the story begins he is serving as a deputy in Congress, representing the left wing of the Peronist party. He married a woman who came to Buenos Aires from the province of Córdoba seeking a professional career, for which there weren't many opportunities in her home town at the time. She completed a secretarial program and got a job as a secretary in the early days of the law firm founded by the man she would marry. After having two children she continued working at the law firm, but she made sure that her children, Catalina and Marco, received a good education at Catholic schools, and she took her family to Mass every Sunday at Basilica San José de Flores. Influenced by the values of her father and her mother, Catalina decided to be a doctor, and after high school she enrolled in medical school at the University of Buenos

Aires, where she had to complete five years of courses plus a year of residency in a hospital in order to be certified for her career.

She is starting her fifth year of medical school when her life is changed radically by a priest, Father Francisco, who has gathered a group of students at the university for a meeting. Father Francisco is the mentor of Young Catholic Students, whose mission is to promote social justice in line with the teachings of the church. With the help of these students and other lay workers, Father Francisco has established a community to serve the poor in one of the slums of Buenos Aires, which appropriately are called *villas miseria*. The slum is located in an area called Bajo Flores, which is south of the neighborhood where Catalina lives. To serve the poor there, the community has built a church, a clinic, and a school. Catalina is impressed by Father Francisco, who conducts the meeting interactively, drawing the students into a conversation about serving the poor. His message resonates with Catalina, whose parents imbued her with the value of service, and with their blessing she signs up to join the community in Bajo Flores.

In the meantime, the political situation in Argentina has been deteriorating. There is social unrest, and a group of urban guerrillas called the Montoneros are committing acts of violence to achieve social justice. Some key members of this group came from Father Francisco's group of Young Catholic Students who decided that, contrary to his teachings, violence was the only way to make the world a better place. The Montoneros are associated with the left wing of the Peronist party, and when the military allows Juan Perón to return to Argentina after years of exile, the Montoneros are at the airport with other left wing followers to greet Perón. But members of the right wing of the party, stationed at the airport as snipers, kill and wound a large number of left wing members of the party. At that point the Montoneros, who are already at war with the military, declare war on the right wing of the Peronist party. The government, encouraged by the military, carries out a program of assassinating leftists, not only the Montoneros but anyone whose mission is to serve the poor. With the death of Perón, his wife becomes president, but as her regime falters, the military tighten their grip on the government, and eventually they stage a coup and take over, initiating a campaign to rid the country of leftists. After Father Francisco is murdered and her father is taken away to a place where no one ever gets out alive, Catalina is drawn into the war, and she plays a key role in a crime against the military that has fatal consequences.

Conversation

As I see it, this novel is about a good person who does something bad. She commits a major crime, a mortal sin, and she can't forgive herself. Society doesn't punish her, she punishers herself.

In a situation she does something that goes against her values, and it has fatal consequences.

The situation is the Dirty War in Argentina during the 1970s when the country was having a civil war between groups on the left and the right, with the military finally exercising authority on behalf of the right. You used this situation in your first published novel, No Way to Peace. *Why did you go back to it?*

In that novel I wrote about five women from different backgrounds and different ethnic groups who had to deal with the war. The situation challenged their values and made them reexamine their lives. In this novel I focus on one woman who got into trouble with the military because of her mission to serve the poor.

Your heroine, Catalina, is in her fifth year of medical school when she volunteers as a lay worker in a clinic established by a priest to serve people in one of the slums of Buenos Aires, which are called villas miseria. *Why did she get into trouble with the military for serving the poor?*

In their minds they regarded people who served the poor as leftists, including the Catholic priests who were serving the poor. In fact, the character of Father Francisco is based on an actual priest who built a church in a *villa miseria* that he called Christ the Worker. Simply the name of that church suggested that he was a Marxist, which put him on the military's list.

It makes me think of Dorothy Day and The Catholic Worker.

Some people regarded her as a dangerous Marxist. Yet she was a devout Catholic, now in the process of being canonized.

From my religious education, I learned that the call to help the poor is deeply embedded in the Judeo-Christian tradition. In both the Old and New Testaments we're exhorted to help strangers, widows, orphans, and generally the poor. So why did some people attack the clergy and lay workers who were implementing these fundamental teachings of the church?

Because the teachings were politicized, as they are now in our country. We even have some clergy now who because of their political mindset take positions against these teachings. At that time in Argentina the clergy were divided between people at higher levels of the church who wanted law and order and people at lower levels who wanted social justice. As an institution the church supported the military because they promised law and order, while many parish priests and lay workers pursued the mission of social justice. As you know, Pope Francis lived through this conflict, and as an archbishop he supported priests and lay workers who were helping the poor in the *villas miseria*.

Your heroine Catalina was born and raised in the neighborhood of Flores, as was Pope Francis, and her family attended the church in Flores that he did. I'm sure this isn't a coincidence.

It isn't a coincidence. She was shaped by where she grew up, as he was. If you lived in Flores, a middle-class neighborhood, you had to be aware of the *villa miseria* in Bajo Flores, just to the south.

Is that why she responded so readily to the call of Father Francisco?

Yes. The desire to serve the poor was already planted in her heart, and Father Francisco brought it to life.

I noticed in your book that the people who lived in those slums were mainly nonwhite people from northern Argentina, Bolivia, and Paraguay. Was there an element of racism in the military's opposition to the priests and lay workers who were serving those people?

Oh, yes. In the minds of the military leaders Argentina was a country for white Europeans.

In some respects, that's not so different from our own country.

No, it's not so different, now that we have a major political party dominated by white nationalists.

You addressed that issue in your novel The Last Resort. *I remember the quotation in the front of the book that came from a paper by one of your students: "Racism is the last resort for people who have failed to build a truly human identity." I think your student was very wise.*

A lot of my students are very wise.

Now, back to Catalina. You show how her mission to serve the poor was affected by the military's actions to suppress people who they regarded as Marxists. They bombed her clinic, they arrested the doctor who was mentoring her for a residency, and they took away her father. Yet she carried on, and she encouraged her community to carry on. In spite of the military's actions against her, she maintained her values, especially the value of nonviolence. She struggled against the temptation to achieve justice through an act of violence. But she finally gave in to the temptation. Why?

At the time she didn't understand why. Though the leader of her group justified the act of violence because it was to raise the money they needed to pursue their mission, she opposed it because it was against their principles. She finally convinced herself that if she participated in the act she could control its outcome and prevent their victim from being harmed.

She spends the rest of her life questioning her motivation because she can't rule out the possibility that she acted in revenge.

That possibility makes it hard to forgive herself.

Well, now she's a doctor, practicing in New York City, operating a clinic in the East Village to serve the poor, so she's living her mission. But is there an element of penance in her mission?

There's an element of penance in the missions of all my protagonists, and you can speculate about what that reveals about me.

I don't need to speculate. I know you. Anyway, she has successfully raised a child, who as an elementary school teacher in south Yonkers is following the family tradition of serving the poor. And then along comes a guy who accosts her as she's leaving her apartment building to go to work and addresses her by the alias she used in her crime. We don't know what he wants from her, but she suspects that he wants revenge.

She does, and her encounter with him stirs up the guilt that she has been living with all those years.

We see that early in the novel. She goes to the local church every morning on her way to work, and she begins her prayer with words from Psalm 51, the Miserere. It helps, but it doesn't absolve her.

It doesn't absolve her because there's something she must do in order to forgive herself. In imaginary conversations with Father Francisco, and in actual conversations with a priest at the local church, she is told what she must do, but she just can't do it.

I don't want to spoil the ending, so I won't comment on what happens. I'll only say, as I said at the beginning of this conversation, the novel is about a good person who does something bad.

That's what it was supposed to be about, but I never know for sure when I start writing a novel. Things always happen.

Discussion questions

1. What do we learn about Catalina from her encounter with the young man in front of her apartment building as she was leaving for work one morning?

2. What do we learn from her encounter with Father Benicio? From her treatment of a patient? From her phone conversation with her daughter? From her dinner with Rachel?

3. What do we learn from her encounter with the young man as she was going home that evening?

4. Growing up in Buenos Aires, what set of values was Catalina given by her family?

5. Why did she go to medical school?

6. Why did she respond so readily to the call from Father Francisco to serve the poor in a *villa miseria*?

7. Why did she so readily adopt Mercedes as her role model?

8. How was she affected by the assassination of Father Francisco?

9. How was she affected by the arrest of Dr. Rosenberg?

10. How did she respond to the bombing of the church, the clinic, and the school?

11. How was she affected by the disappearance of her father?

12. Why did she decide to stay in Buenos Aires instead of going to Rio Cuarto with her mother?

13. Though she knew it was wrong, why did she decide to play a role in the kidnapping of Colonel Yribarren?

14. What was her mental state after she saw what the military had done to her group at the quinta?

15. How did she build a new life in America on the wreckage of her old life in Argentina?

16. What were the main features of her new identity in America?

17. Was there an element of penance in her continuing mission to serve the poor in New York City?

18. What did she learn about her crime from her conversations with Mercedes? With Father Francisco? With her mother? With Father Benicio? With Rachel?

19. With all the encouragement that she received from other people, why was she unable to forgive herself for her role in the kidnapping?

20. What did she finally learn from her conversation with Ricardo Morales?